HIDE AND SEEK

Hand in hand Rachel and Esth[...]
secret cabinet.

The doorbell rings. Rachel h[...]
door and then voices speaking in German.

"No," says Aunt Nel. "I haven't seen them. They must be somewhere else."

"Nazis," cries Esther. "I hear Nazis."

They hear the outside door close.

"They're inside, Rachel. They're inside."

Rachel squeezes Esther's hand. Esther squeezes back.

It is very still in the house. They don't hear anyone. "They're inside," Rachel thinks. "They're going to shoot through the cabinet now." She feels her whole body beginning to shake.

Then . . . a shot.

"This fictionalized account tells of the childhood experiences of the author, a Dutch poet, during World War II, including the bombing of Rotterdam by the Germans. The understated prose and graceful translation make it both compelling and accessible to young readers."   — *New York Times Book Review*

OTHER PUFFIN BOOKS ABOUT WORLD WAR II

Hide and Seek

Ida Vos

*Translated by Terese Edelstein
and Inez Smidt*

PUFFIN BOOKS

PUFFIN BOOKS
Published by the Penguin Group
Penguin Books USA Inc., 375 Hudson Street, New York, New York 10014, U.S.A.
Penguin Books Ltd, 27 Wrights Lane, London W8 5TZ, England
Penguin Books Australia Ltd, Ringwood, Victoria, Australia
Penguin Books Canada Ltd, 10 Alcorn Avenue, Toronto, Ontario, Canada M4V 3B2
Penguin Books (N.Z.) Ltd, 182-190 Wairau Road, Auckland 10, New Zealand

Penguin Books Ltd, Registered Offices: Harmondsworth, Middlesex, England

First published in the Netherlands as *Wie Niet Weg Is Wordt Gezien* by Uitgeverij Leopold, 1981

First published in the United States of America by Houghton Mifflin Company, 1991
Reprinted by arrangement with Houghton Mifflin Company
Published in Puffin Books, 1995

1 3 5 7 9 10 8 6 4 2

LIBRARY OF CONGRESS CATALOGING-IN-PUBLICATION DATA
Vos, Ida.
[Wie niet weg is wordt gezien. English]
Hide and seek / Ida Vos ; translated by Terese Edelstein and Inez Smidt.
p. cm.
"First published in the Netherlands . . . 1981"—T.p. verso.
Summary: A young Jewish girl living in Holland tells of her
experiences during the Nazi occupation, her years in hiding,
and the aftershock when the war finally ends.
ISBN 0-14-036908-2
1. World War, 1939-1945—Netherlands—Juvenile fiction.
[1. World War, 1939-1945—Netherlands—Fiction. 2. World War, 1939-1945—Jews—Rescue—Fiction.
3. Netherlands—History—German occupation, 1940-1945—Fiction.
4. Jews—Netherlands—Fiction.] I. Edelstein, Terese. II. Smidt, Inez.
III. Title.
PZ7.V9718Hi   1995   [Fic]—dc20   94-30193   CIP   AC

Printed in the United States of America

*To our wartime foster parents
Aunt Nel and Uncle Jaap De Lange*

Come with me.

Come with me to a small country in Western Europe. To the Netherlands, a land also known as Holland.

Come with me, back to the year 1940.

I am eight years old.

German soldiers are parading through the Dutch streets. They have helmets on their heads and they are wearing black boots. They are marching and singing songs that have words I don't understand.

"They're going to kill all the Jews!" shouts my mother.

I am afraid, I have a stomachache.

I am Jewish.

The Germans come up with all sorts of things to make life difficult for us.

Suddenly, I am no longer allowed to attend my own school. I am not allowed to go swimming or to play tennis. I am not allowed to go to the library or the movies or to sit outside on a bench. I am not allowed to take a train or to go to a park.

The black-and-white signs are everywhere: FORBIDDEN FOR JEWS.

I am not allowed to do anything, and I have to wear a yellow Star of David on my clothes. In the middle of the star is the word *Jew.* Now everyone can see that I am a Jewish child.

I no longer dare to go outside.

The Germans have put my grandparents in a camp.

"They must work hard there," my father says.

I don't believe him. They are already so old. My grandpa is seventy-four. My grandma is seventy-one.

I feel that something dreadful is going to happen to them. But I don't know what.

Because we don't want to go to a camp, we hide from the Germans. That is called "being in hiding." We may no longer go outside, and we must be very quiet. No one is supposed to know where we are and no one is supposed to hear us.

My little sister and I drill a tiny hole through an outside door. In this way we can see what is happening out on the street. First she may look with one eye through the hole, then I may have a turn.

I am angry. I am afraid.

Suddenly it is over. It is May 1945, and I am allowed to go outside again. American and Canadian soldiers have come to chase the Germans away.

I may go to school again. I am thirteen years old and I am only in the fifth grade. How stupid I became when I was in hiding.

I may go swimming again, I may go to the library, I may sit on a bench again. I may spend the night away from home.

I want to go visit my grandparents, but I can't. I can't visit my cousins Marga and Mientje, either, for they are all dead. They were killed because they were Jews.

I can no longer visit . . .

I won't go on. After the war there were so many people who were dead. Too many to tell you about in this foreword.

Can you imagine how it feels when you find out that people you love are dead, all of a sudden?

Imagine what it would be like not ever to be allowed to go outside, year after year. Imagine being able to do your shopping only between three and five o'clock. Imagine . . .

I know how difficult it is to imagine such things; that is the reason I wrote *Hide and Seek*. To let you feel how terrible it is to be discriminated against, and to let you know how terrible it was to be a Jewish child in Holland during those years.

When you have finished reading *Hide and Seek,* I want you to go outside for a while, if that is possible. Breathe deeply, play, shout.

Be happy! Be free!

Ida Vos
Rijswijk, Holland
Spring 1990

❖ Reading

There is a new girl in the class. Her name is Akke. Akke cannot read well, and now Miss Koetsveld has asked Rachel Hartog if she wants to help Akke.

"Rachel," the teacher said, "you already can read well. During a free afternoon would you like to practice a little bit with Akke? She lives very close to you."

"That would be fun, Miss Koetsveld," Rachel answered. She is proud that she will be allowed to help Akke. Rachel knew her letters by the time she was five. That is why she is bored sometimes when the other children in the class must read aloud.

Today is not as boring as usual. A new picture is hanging on the classroom wall. "Beatrix, one year old" is written on it. You see a photo of a plump little girl in a playpen. The little girl is a princess and her parents are Princess Juliana and Prince Bernhard. Rachel has to smile when she looks at that chubby baby. It helps prevent boredom.

Today is Wednesday. School is over for the day at quarter past eleven. Next year, when Rachel is in the third grade, she will go home at twelve o'clock, but now she gets out of school nice and early.

"Are you coming this afternoon?" Rachel asks Akke.

"If my mother lets me."

"Good, see you this afternoon then. I live at Viruly-plein Thirteen-A."

Rachel is waiting for Akke now. She has gathered together a pile of books in her room. Akke may choose which book she wants to read.

There is the bell. Rachel runs downstairs to open the door.

"Hello," she says to Akke, who is standing on the pavement. "Come in, we'll go upstairs.

"This is my room," Rachel announces.

"Pretty," says Akke. "I sleep with my little brother and little sister in one room. We have six children in our family."

Together they sit on Rachel's bed. They read about Ot and Sien and Pim and Mien. It is very cozy. When they have finished a book, Akke takes another one.

"What's that now? Do I have to read *that* one?" Akke looks in surprise at a book that she has in her hands.

Rachel can't help laughing at Akke. "Oh, no, those aren't Dutch letters. Those are Hebrew letters. Jewish people often read Hebrew."

"Crazy," remarks Akke. "Who would ever want to read Hebrew?"

"Jews," Rachel answers.

*   *   *

When they come to school the next day Miss Koetsveld says, "Well — did you get together? Did you read together yesterday afternoon?"

"Yes, Miss Koetsveld," replies Akke.

"Will you go to Rachel's house again on Wednesday afternoon?"

"No, Miss Koetsveld."

"No? The next Wednesday, then?" asks Miss Koetsveld.

"No, never again," answers Akke.

"Never again? Why not?"

"My father won't let me read Jewish books."

❖ *Blackout*

"Don't be frightened," Father says. "Tonight we'll be having a blackout drill." Blackout drill? Rachel doesn't understand.

"Tonight at nine o'clock all the lights outside will go out," Father explains. "Not a single light may shine from inside the houses, either. This is a trial run in case there should be a war. If the lights are on, the enemy can see where Rotterdam is, and that is very dangerous, for then the enemy could bomb the city."

Rachel still does not know what to think about the blackout, but she knows it must be something very bad. She can see that on Father's face.

All day long Rachel senses that something terrible will be happening tonight. She is aware of it even when she is playing with her dolls. It remains with her the entire day, that nasty feeling.

"May I stay up?" Esther asks when it is nearly half past seven.

"Nothing doing," Mother replies. "Tomorrow you have to go to nursery school again, and you must be well rested. Have an apple and then off to bed with you."

"How can Mother be so cheerful?" Rachel thinks.

Father is not at all cheerful. "Tonight is the dress rehearsal," he keeps saying, and then he sighs.

Rachel does not know what a dress rehearsal is, but she knows it must be something awful. She can hear that in Father's voice.

At half past seven their parents put Esther and Rachel to bed. "Sleep well," Papa says.

"Be good," adds Mama, "and sweet dreams."

"I don't want to go to sleep," Rachel whines.

"Hold your tongue and remember, no lights on. Tonight we must be in the dark," her father warns.

Rachel lies in the dark with her eyes wide open. Through the closed curtains she sees the lights of the street lamps. Soon the lamps will no longer give off light, and then she'll be alone in the dark. She puts her head under the covers. Since it is already dark there, she won't notice when the lights outside are extinguished.

It is becoming oppressive under the blankets. Rachel pokes her head out from under the covers, but she can't sleep. She keeps opening her eyes to see if it is dark outside yet.

Suddenly it happens. There is no light anymore, anywhere. Soon the trolls and the werewolves and the evil dwarfs will come and pull her out of bed. Rachel is becoming soaked with sweat, just as she was a couple of months ago when she had a fever.

Rachel gets out of bed. She wants to go downstairs to Papa and Mama. She walks down the stairs carefully. She is not allowed to turn the light on; she knows that well enough. They must not let the enemy know where people live.

Rachel is at the door to the living room now. Very soon she can go sit in Papa's or Mama's lap. She opens the door quietly. There is no one in the dark room. Papa and Mama are gone! But they knew about the dress rehearsal, didn't they?

"How very dark it is outside. I hope this never becomes

a reality." That was Papa's voice. Papa and Mama are outside!

With only her nightgown on, Rachel runs into the street. "Where are you?" she calls out. She feels Mama's arms around her.

"What's the matter, little one?" Mama asks.

"You shouldn't leave me. It's so dark," Rachel whimpers.

"Silly girl," Mama answers. "We're not leaving you."

"Not even if the enemy comes?"

"Not even if the enemy comes."

"Is the enemy coming?"

"Go to sleep. I'll put you back to bed."

❖ *Die Fahnen hoch!*

The Hartogs are standing among many people on the Beukelsdijk. Soldiers in strange uniforms are walking with outstretched legs along the road. They are swinging their legs high in the air and are singing a German song, *"Die Fahnen hoch,"* which means "The Banners High."

It sounds rather nice. In any case, it is better than the sounds of airplanes and of bombs and sirens. It is silent in the air now; no bombs are falling anymore. "The Netherlands has capitulated. We have surrendered to the Germans," Mr. Hartog says, and he looks very unhappy. "This marching is only the beginning."

The road becomes more and more crowded. People are continually arriving to watch. They stand motionless on the side of the road with grave looks on their faces. The soldiers are waving. Occasionally someone in the crowd waves back. Rachel can hear very clearly that the German soldiers have iron under their boots. Each time they put their feet down on the ground she hears the sound of metal on brick. It makes a horrible noise.

One man in the crowd begins to shout loudly. "Rotten Germans!" he cries out. "You have burned the heart of the city. Everything is gone because of your bombs. The Hoogstraat, the Kipstraat, the Grote Markt, everything is burning. I was there this morning. I saw it. You have murdered Rotterdam!" The man is weeping now.

"Shhh," admonish the people standing near him. "Not so loud. They'll hear you."

"They'll hear me? Of course they'll hear me. They *must* hear me!" The man cries even louder. He can't stop.

Rachel has never seen anything like this. She is eight years old, but she has never, ever heard anyone cry so loudly in the street.

Esther, who is only five years old, is frightened. She pulls on Father's shirt. "I want my mama," she says.

"We'll go in a minute," her father replies. "Don't be scared. These Germans won't do anything. They don't have any bombs."

"I want to go, too," Rachel says. "I've had enough of those soldiers."

"Just a minute, Rachel. We'll go soon."

"*Die Fahnen hoch!*" the soldiers sing, and they keep on marching.

Behind them someone shouts, "Come home, David, Esther, Rachel. They'll murder us!"

There is Mother. She is still wearing her apron. Her hair has not been combed, and her eyes are wide open. Rachel has never seen her mother look like this. She can no longer understand what Mother is shouting; she hears only Mother's screams above the sound of the boots.

"Stop. Get hold of yourself," Father says firmly while he grasps Mother by her shoulders. "Stop!"

"They are singing '*Die Fahnen hoch!*'" Mother shrieks. "They are singing a Nazi song."

"Calm down. They won't do anything to us." Father puts his arms around Mother and presses her against him. "Calm down. Calm down."

The boots stamp on and on.

"They're singing another German song, '*Die Reihen fest geschlossen,*'" Mother shouts. "It means 'The Rows Close Together.' They're going to kill all the Jews."

"They're not going to do anything to us," Father says to console her.

"That's what Uncle Erich and Uncle Joseph thought, too, in 1938. Until a thousand stones were thrown through the windows of their shops and they had to flee to Holland."

"That was in Germany. Such a thing won't happen in Holland," Father says.

Mother is still crying. People come and stand around her. "Come with me," a man says. "I'll give her a few sedatives from my pharmacy."

They enter the pharmacy. The pharmacist goes to a big bottle that is full of pills. He shakes two pills out of the bottle into his hand. "Take these," he says to Rachel's mother. "I'll get you a glass of water." Mother doesn't look at the pills.

"Take them," the pharmacist urges. "They're harmless. They won't kill you."

"No?"

"No."

"That's too bad," says Mother.

❖ Cross-eyed Chicken

"Rachel, are you coming? We have to go!"

Leo stands at the bottom of the stairs. Leo is Rachel's cousin, and he has promised to come get her because it is so difficult to go to a different school for the first time all by yourself.

The Hartogs are living in Rijswijk now, close to Leo and Bob and Uncle Jacob and Aunt Sari. Mama doesn't want to live in Rotterdam any longer because such a large part of the city has been destroyed by the German bombs. "I can't bear it," Mama often said. "All those wrecked houses where people were living such a short time ago. All those blackened trees, it hurts me to look at them. I want to move to Rijswijk. I want to live close to my brother."

That is why Rachel has to go to a different school today, and that is the reason Leo is yelling for her at the bottom of the stairs.

Rachel is a little bit afraid of Leo. He is a year older than she is. He is strong and heavy and he likes to tease people. When she began wearing glasses, Leo often called her "cross-eyed chicken," and she is worried that he will do it again now. Having to go to a new school and then being called names — all this is not so easy to take.

"I'm coming," she calls to Leo. "'Bye, Mama. I'm going."

"'Bye, Rachel. Have a good time. See you later and take care!"

When they are near the school, Rachel stands still for a moment.

"Keep walking," says Leo as he gives her a little push on her back. "Otherwise we'll be late."

The children playing in the school yard are running every which way. "You're 'it,'" a big boy says as he taps Leo on the shoulder.

"I'm not playing, Jan," Leo says. "I'm going to stay with my cousin. She is new and she is from Rotterdam."

"From Rotterdam? Did bombs fall on your head?" the boy asks Rachel.

"No, they didn't," she wants to say, but Leo is quicker.

"And how!" he replies. "Do you see that one eye of hers?"

"Here it comes," Rachel thinks. "Now he is going to call me 'cross-eyed chicken.'"

"That one eye," Leo continues. "Do you know why that eye turns in a little?"

"No, why?"

"Because of the bombing. A bomb has so much air pressure that it can make your eyes get twisted in your head."

"Boys," Jan calls, "come here, everybody! This is Leo's

cousin. She is new, and we'll let her become a member of our secret club right away, for something terrific has happened to her. She has something very special. Do you see that one eye of hers? It turns in because of the bombing in Rotterdam."

Rachel is so embarrassed because of all those children that she would like to run home. But Leo whispers something into her ear.

"That was good, wasn't it? Cross-eyed chicken!"

❖ *Counting-off Rhyme*

> This is what I have to say,
> Hitler, Hitler go away,
> Hitler is a big fat swine,
> You are "it" this time.

This is the new counting-off rhyme Rachel has just learned. Nobody knows where it came from, but it certainly is fun to sing. Rachel sings it whenever she plays hide-and-seek with the other Jewish children. They have agreed to sing the song only when no strangers are around. Imagine that an N.S.B.-er, a member of the

Dutch Nazi Party, should hear it; such a person might become furious and tell the Germans about it. "Jewish children are playing over there," he would say. "They are calling Hitler names."

There are no strangers nearby this Wednesday afternoon, so the children feel free to use the Hitler counting-off rhyme. "This is what I have to say, Hitler, Hitler go away!" they shout.

Maybe it helps to shout the rhyme. Maybe Hitler really will die. "Remember, if someone we don't know comes close, we'll say 'Eeny, meeny, miney, mo,' like we used to," Herman says. Herman is a neighbor who is also Jewish.

"Hitler is a big fat swine. You're 'it.' "

"Look out!" Herman calls. "Here comes Hilde." Hilde's father is an N.S.B.-er. You never know what she might do.

"Hello, can I play, too?" Hilde asks.

The children look at one another. No one says a word.

"It looks like you're having so much fun. I want to play, too."

"Eeny, meeny, miney, mo," the Jewish children sing.

"No, not that rhyme," Hilde says. "That other rhyme. The one about Hitler."

"All right," Herman says with a sigh. "We'll see what happens."

Hilde sings as loudly as they do. "Hitler is a big fat swine."

"It's strange," Rachel thinks. "It's strange that Hilde wants to play with us. Maybe she thinks Hitler is a big fat swine, too."

"Hilde, what are you doing there?" A woman is standing next to Hilde. She has a stern face, and when Rachel looks lower down she can see that the woman is wearing a brooch on the collar of her coat. It is a three-cornered pin with a lion on it, and surrounding that lion are three letters: N.S.B.

"Hilde, answer me. What are you doing there?"

"I'm not doing anything, Grandma. I'm playing."

"Go home!" shouts her grandmother. "My granddaughter is insulting the Führer together with Jewish children. Disgraceful, I'm going to tell your parents!"

Hilde does not want to leave, but her grandmother is strong. She pulls the child along by the arm. "Hurry up. Go home, I tell you!"

The other children continue with their play:

> Eeny, meeny, miney, mo,
> Catch a tiger by the toe,
> If he hollers let him go,
> Eeny, meeny, miney, mo.

❖ Hide-and-Seek

Rachel finds it wonderful to play outside these days. While she is playing she can talk about the past, when she was still allowed to be in the same class with non-Jewish children.

But that is no longer allowed. The Germans have assigned the Jewish children to a school in the Bezemstraat in the center of The Hague.

While playing outside Rachel hears what the non-Jewish children at her former school have been doing.

"We had a history test," says Johan. "I got a D."

"Boy, is arithmetic hard! We have to learn fractions," Martin complains.

"Fractions? What are those?" asks Rachel. "Do you have to fracture something?"

"Too difficult to explain. I don't understand it myself," says Marieke.

Sometimes the non-Jewish children forget that Rachel no longer attends their school. They say things to each other that she does not comprehend at all.

"Too bad that we couldn't play 'around the world' in gym class today. Miss Terlet was in a bad mood," Klaartje grumbles. "But it was sort of our own fault."

"Yes, it was," one of the other children agrees.

What are they talking about? Rachel thinks. "Never mind, I'm not going to ask."

"We're going to play hide-and-seek. Rachel, you're 'it'!"

Rachel puts her hands in front of her eyes. "Ten, twenty, thirty . . . eighty, ninety, one hundred! Ready or not, here I come!"

Rachel looks into the empty street. There is not a child to be seen. She will have to go searching now.

Rachel looks behind the little wall. She looks under the bench. She looks behind the tree. "They've certainly found some good hiding places," she whispers to herself.

A child is laughing in the distance. Marieke laughs like that. Rachel walks toward the park. The laughter is becoming clearer.

"Shhh, here she comes," Rachel hears someone say. She takes a few steps into the park. They are probably over there behind that thick oak tree.

All of a sudden Rachel sees the white board with black letters, the board that she has seen so often already. The words FORBIDDEN FOR JEWS are written upon it.

Rachel can no longer play hide-and-seek; it is forbidden by the Nazis. Only non-Jewish children may play that game. She walks out of the park. She will go home and read a book. Reading has not been forbidden to her.

"One, two, three, home free!" calls Johan.

"One, two, three, home free!" calls Marieke.

❖ Would You Like a Star, Too?

Today for the first time Rachel must go to school with a yellow star on her coat, a big yellow star, with the word *Jew* written in the middle of it. Thus everyone can see that she is Jewish. The Germans have ordered the wearing of the star, and Rachel finds it horrible.

All her mother did yesterday evening was sew stars on their clothing. "I see stars," Mother said, and they even had to laugh about it.

"I'll take you to the tram," says Papa. "Come on, hurry up, otherwise you'll be late for school."

They put their coats on. How big the star is. Esther's star is even bigger than Rachel's. "It looks that way because Esther has such a small body," their father explains. "That's why her star seems larger."

When they arrive at the tram stop they see many other people with stars on, grown-up people and little people. "All Jews," an old man says. "Yesterday I did not know they were Jews, although I suspected they were."

"You must hold your schoolbag under your arm as you usually do, not against your star," Father admonishes her.

Rachel blushes. Father saw that she was trying to hide her star.

"It's difficult, but if you don't hide your star now, you'll get over the embarrassment more quickly. When the war is over, we'll make a huge fire and we'll throw all the stars of the whole world into it."

"Boy, will that stink!" Rachel exclaims.

"It stinks right now," Leo says. "I smelled the star when I put my coat on."

"Children, here comes the tram," Father calls.

The moment has come. For the first time Rachel will have to go on the tram with that horrible star.

"Come in!" the driver of the tram calls out to them. "It really is springtime in my tram now. All these children with yellow daffodils on their coats. I wish I could wear one."

When they are all inside, many people begin to clap, just as an audience does at the end of a play. Rachel does not understand. A man nudges her. "Bow, the clapping is for you, for your stars."

Rachel does not dare to move. What is that? Are the people clapping for that big yellow star?

The children look at one another. "They are clapping for us," Leo says, and he begins to bow. "Thank you, people. Thank you very much."

A few people do not clap, but look straight ahead instead. Leo approaches one of those people. "Ma'am, would you like a star, too? Tomorrow I'll bring you one. Would you like a star, too, mister?"

"Go away, you little Jew boy," the man replies, and to the woman sitting next to him he says, "You can't cut them down to size. Not the big Jews and not the little ones, either."

❖ *Bicycles*

How happy Rachel was when she received a new bicycle on her birthday. A real bicycle with white tires and with a lot of shining chrome.

At first Rachel continually stepped off to see if there was any mud on the finish. If she saw even one speck, she would take her handkerchief and would spit on it a little. Then she would wipe the mud off.

Rachel is still happy with the bicycle, but not so very much anymore. She must turn it in. Next week all bicycles must be brought to the police station. Jews may no longer have bicycles.

Rachel finds it terrible, and she often thinks about the German child who will be riding her bicycle. She always becomes very unhappy then, and she does her best to think about something else.

"Tomorrow is the day," says Father. "Take the basket off your bicycle. They don't have to have that."

"Don't I have to go with you, David?" asks Mother.

"No. I can ride with two bicycles at the same time, and perhaps Rachel wants to see her own bicycle off."

"Yes, Papa, we'll go together," Rachel says.

They now stand outside the door of their house. Each of Father's hands rests on a bicycle. "Come, let's go," he says.

Father mounts his bicycle. He rides with one hand and steers Mother's bicycle with the other. "Come on," he calls.

Rachel gets on her bicycle. They can't ride next to each other because it is much too dangerous. Three bicycles side by side are too many.

When they arrive at the police station, they see many other people there with bicycles. They form a line. A police officer comes to the doorway. He has a red face and very, very blue eyes.

"Next!" calls the policeman.

"Papa, that's no German," Rachel exclaims.

"No, dear, that's a Dutchman. He is helping the Germans."

After fifteen minutes it is their turn.

"This way." The Dutchman points.

"Must I carry those bicycles upstairs myself?" asks Father.

"Yes, you dirty little Jew, two flights up," answers the policeman.

"Villain," whispers Father.

"Did you say something?" asks the police officer.

"No," Father replies.

"Rachel," says Father, "keep your little bike with you. I'll bring the big bicycles first, and then yours."

Father takes Mother's bicycle first. When he comes downstairs a couple of minutes later, he is breathing very quickly. "Wouldn't you rather wait outside?" he asks.

"No, Papa, I'll stay here."

When Father has taken his own bicycle upstairs, it is time for her bicycle to go.

"Give it here," says Father. "There is nothing to be done. It can't be any other way."

Rachel strokes the brown saddle. "Goodbye, bicycle!" she calls. "So long, bicycle!"

Father is on the second flight of stairs now. Rachel can hear that, but she doesn't see him anymore. Actually she can't see anything, for tears are running from her eyes. Tears are coming from her nose, too. It is wicked, wicked! Those Germans are ugly bicycle thieves — that's what they are!

Suddenly there is a terrible noise upstairs. It sounds like a thunderstorm.

"As if I can help it," Rachel hears Papa call out. "I tripped."

Rachel runs up the steps. Her bicycle is lying in a hallway. The wheels are spinning in the air. They are no longer round.

"Hurry up," orders a policeman. "And take your daughter with you!"

They rush down the stairs. "That was something," says Father when they are standing outside.

"Did you trip?" Rachel asks.

"Well, no, my girl. Suddenly I became so terribly angry about that bicycle of yours that I could do nothing but throw it downstairs."

"You are a hero," exclaims Rachel.

"Oh, oh, oh," Father says with a little laugh. "Your bicycle almost fell on a policeman. Too bad he didn't get it on his thick head."

❖ *Stomachache in the Night*

"Rachel!"

Rachel pulls the covers over her head. She has been sound asleep. She doesn't want to get up.

"Rachel!" Mother pulls the covers back. "I need you. Papa is sick."

Rachel is already out of bed. She goes to her parents'

bedroom with her mother. Father is lying in the big bed. He has a strange expression on his face and is kicking his legs about.

"I can't stand it anymore," he moans. "I have such a stomachache. I think it's something very bad."

"Shall I get you a hot water bottle?" Mother asks.

"No, don't bother. You'll have to get a doctor."

"Dear David, you know I can't go outside. The Nazis have forbidden us to leave our house between eight o'clock in the evening and six o'clock in the morning. You know that, don't you, or have you forgotten it because of the pain?"

"I'm going to die!" Father whispers.

"Is papa really going to die, Mama?" Rachel asks fearfully.

"Oh, no, child, Father is being a little bit touchy, that's all."

Father is lying quite still now. He is very white and he is breathing rapidly. "A doctor, Ruth . . . a doctor."

Rachel looks at Papa. She knows for sure that he's going to die tonight; she will no longer have a father then.

"I'll open the window," says Mama. "Perhaps someone will come by who can fetch a doctor for us."

Mother pushes up the window and leans way out. "There is someone," she says. "A woman."

"Maybe she'll come closer," says Rachel hopefully.

"Yes, there she is," exclaims Mother. "I'm going to call her now.

"Ma'am, ma'am! Yes, I'm up here. Would you listen for a moment? My husband is terribly sick. Would you please fetch a doctor for us?"

"Of course," calls the woman. "Which doctor shall I fetch?"

"You see, ma'am, we're not allowed to go outside."

"You're not allowed to go outside? Why not?"

"We're Jews, and Jews must remain in their homes from eight o'clock in the evening until six o'clock the next morning!"

The woman looks at her watch. "In two hours it will be six o'clock," she calls out. "Then you can fetch the doctor yourself."

❖ *Birthday*

"Esther, that green streamer must go there, above by the light," Rachel orders.

The girls are decorating the room together, for tomorrow is Mother's birthday. When it is someone's birthday you must have decorations, war or no war.

For days the two children had thought about what they should give their mother, and this afternoon they set out to buy something. They would rather have gone in the morning, but that is not allowed. Jews must do their shopping at three o'clock, and they may not even shop for as long as they want. Ready or not, they must leave the stores at five o'clock.

At the stroke of three Rachel and Esther entered the store where you could buy all sorts of things. Dinner plates and watering cans and much more.

"I think that's a pretty cup. Shall we buy that for Mama, Rachel?" Esther asked. "What is written on the cup, Rachel?"

Esther can't read yet, so Rachel read aloud the writing on the cup: " 'For my dear mama' is on the cup, Esther."

"Good, we'll buy it. How much does it cost?" Esther inquired.

"One guilder thirty," the saleswoman answered, and when she said that she looked very quickly at the stars on the girls' coats. Rachel thought the woman was nice, because she knew for sure that the woman said one guilder thirty on account of the star. The cup was certainly much more expensive.

They are finished decorating now. Rachel takes a piece of soap and in beautiful letters she writes on the mirror:

"Hooray, it's Mama's birthday."

How festive it will be tomorrow, even though it will be different from last year. Aunt Esther and Uncle Max will not be there, and neither will Mirjam and Sally. They have simply disappeared.

"Gone," say Father and Mother, and "gone" is something very bad.

Grandpa and Grandma from Mama's side will not be coming, either. They would have to travel by train, and that is forbidden to Jews. Jews must ask permission from the Germans, and the Germans really will not say: "Yes ma'am, yes sir, go right ahead."

They won't do that for a birthday.

Grandpa and Grandma from Papa's side will be coming. Luckily they don't live so far away. Papa will go fetch them. Grandpa doesn't walk too well. He is already very old.

Mama has baked a cake, for Grandma loves cake. Cake is nice and soft, and Grandma can no longer chew very well.

The next morning they awaken early. They go to Papa's and Mama's bedroom.

"Happy birthday, Mama," Rachel says.

"And many more happy returns," says Esther. "Here is our present."

Mama unwraps the cup. "How pretty," she says. "I would like to give a cup just like this one to Papa's mother when she comes this afternoon."

"At three o'clock Esther and I will go buy a cup for Grandma. Is that all right?" asks Rachel.

"Yes, please," says Mother.

At three o'clock Rachel and Esther are on their way. When they get back, Grandpa and Grandma will be there. Father has already left to get them.

When the girls come home they set the cup in front of Grandma's place at the table, next to the cake. They wait impatiently for Papa to come with Grandpa and Grandma. It is taking a very long time.

"Do you want a piece of cake?" asks Esther.

"No, we'll wait until everyone is here," answers Rachel. "Then the real party will begin. Keep your hands off. Don't pick at the cake."

Many minutes have gone by when the children finally hear the key in the lock of the door. They run to the steps to greet Grandpa and Grandma. "Ha . . . are you . . ." they scream.

Father is alone. He walks up the steps very slowly. "They're gone," he says. "They have been taken out of their house by the Germans. They're gone. Gone!"

❖ Bench

Rachel is not allowed to go swimming. Not because she is sick; oh, no, not because of that. The Germans have forbidden it. That is the way it is nowadays for Jewish children.

Rachel is allowed to roller skate, so that is what she does. She was given the skates for no reason at all. It was not even her birthday, not yet, anyway, but nevertheless she has eight shining wheels under her feet now.

At first she didn't skate very well, but it is going much better now. Sometimes she can even skate on one leg, and that is very difficult to do.

Her skating is going well today. Rachel has skated up and down the same stretch about twenty times now. Near her house is a canal, and along that canal is a very long sidewalk. If she skates on this sidewalk she doesn't have to cross any streets, and that is good, for she is afraid of falling down on the cobblestones.

After Rachel has been skating a while she goes to sit on a bench. "Oh!" she sighs. "How nice it is to sit down when you're tired."

She looks around. It is beautiful outside. The leaves on the trees are turning slightly yellow. The ducks that were hatched this summer have gotten big. They are growing too, just as she is, only a bit faster.

"Rachel!" She looks across the road. Tineke has called her.

"Hello!" Rachel calls back. "Where are you going?"

Immediately she realizes that there was no need to ask. Tineke has a towel under her arm. She is going swimming, of course.

"To the swimming pool," Tineke replies. "Are you coming?"

"I'm not allowed to go!"

"Maybe your mother will let you go swimming tomorrow!"

Rachel does not answer. There is no reason for Tineke to know that it is not her mother who has forbidden it, but the Germans.

Rachel sits on the bench a while longer. Then she sees her mother, who is coming out of the house with a big shopping bag on her arm. "Stop, Mama, I'll come with you!" she calls. She likes to go shopping with Mama. Actually, it is nicer than playing outside. She will go skating again tomorrow, and the day after tomorrow.

Before Rachel goes outside the next day, Mama stops her. "Wait a minute, Rachel. I have something to tell you. Starting today we are not allowed to sit outside on a bench. The Germans have forbidden it. You know what can happen if you disobey the Germans, don't you?"

"Yes, Mama." Rachel sighs. The announcement must have appeared in the special newspaper, the one that is only for Jews. Again there is something else they are not allowed to do, and there is nothing to be done about it. She will sit down on the ground when she has to put her roller skates on and take them off. If she should sit on a bench, the whole family could be arrested, and she doesn't want that.

Just as she did on the previous day, Rachel is skating on the sidewalk alongside the canal. It looks as though the young ducks have grown even bigger. They are swimming behind a large duck. Is that the father or the mother? Oh, look over there . . .

"Ow!" she yells. Rachel doesn't know how it happened, but suddenly she is sitting on the ground. She has a terrible pain in her knee. A red puddle has formed on the pavement. "Mama!" she shouts. "Mama, I'm bleeding!"

"Come on," says a man who has seen what happened. "Come on, I'll help you get up. Come, we'll go sit down on the bench and then we'll see what the matter is with your knee."

"Don't! Don't!" Rachel screams.

"Don't be such a sissy. Come on, let's go sit on the bench." He would like to put Rachel down on the bench, but she knows that she can't sit there. She tries to bite the man. She takes hold of his hand and bites down on a finger as hard as she can.

"Rotten girl!" the man calls out as he puts his finger in his mouth. "Stubborn, rotten girl!" He stalks away.

Rachel is sitting on the sidewalk in front of the bench. She is crying, but she is very glad that big man was unable to put her down on the bench. Imagine that! It is absolutely forbidden by the Germans.

"Stupid man!" she would like to shout. "Stupid man! Don't you know that Jewish children aren't allowed to do anything!"

❖ *The Eternal Jew*

Since the Nazis no longer allow Rachel to take the tram to school, she walks each day with a group of children from Rijswijk to The Hague. It is rather pleasant to walk together with so many children. They talk to one another, play tag, and look at the shop windows along the Rijswijkseweg. Every day they stop in front of one particular window. It is a shop where festive noses and masks are sold. The children would like to go inside, but that isn't possible. At half past seven and at half past one Jews aren't allowed to enter shops, not even novelty shops.

Rachel always falls behind the others when they pass the fire station, for there is something gruesome to see. The Germans have hung a picture there, a very horrible one. It is the head of a Jew with vicious eyes. His mouth has a tooth protruding from it, and there is a Star of David drawn on his forehead. Rachel can't see his hands, but surely they are not hands, but claws. Above his head is written in phony Hebrew letters "The Eternal Jew," and underneath the picture: "You too should see this film!"

Rachel doesn't want to look at that monstrous face, but she looks nevertheless, with one eye. Then it doesn't seem quite so hideous.

Rachel has often looked at Jews since the picture appeared. Nobody has such a face and such claws. She doesn't have them, either. She has tried to make a face like that in the mirror, but she can't do it.

She calls the man in the picture "The Scary Jew," but she doesn't tell that to anyone, not even Max, who sits behind her at school. Each time she has to pass the picture, she gets the urge to scrape off a tiny bit with her fingernail, until the entire picture disappears. Then the Nazis would say: "Where is the Eternal Jew? We shall be on the lookout to see who damaged it, and when we find the guilty person, we'll arrest him." They would do that, too, for anyone who damages property belonging to the Nazis is punished.

Today the children don't gossip as they usually do on their way to school. It is terribly cold and it is raining. Rachel was allowed to take Mama's umbrella, but an umbrella can protect her only from the rain, not from the cold.

She watches the tram that is passing by. Oh, how she would like to take the tram to school, but she isn't allowed to do that. Jewish children have to walk, day in and day out.

The rain makes a tapping sound on the umbrella. The rain streams down along the face of the Eternal Jew. Rachel gazes at him with one eye. It seems that he is calling out to her, "See, this is what we look like now!"

Rachel walks past the picture. She feels her umbrella touching it, and then notices a wet piece of paper on one of the umbrella spokes. She looks at the picture again. "You too should see . . ." it says. The rest of the sentence is hanging on the umbrella.

Rachel has an idea. What if she should walk once again past the picture and go once again with the spokes of the umbrella along that evil face, on purpose this time?

Rachel walks on tiptoe so that the umbrella is high enough to touch a tooth or the eyes.

It worked! She has reached the eyes. The Eternal Jew is blind now. He can't look at her anymore. She runs to school.

"Go sit down," Mr. Noach says to Rachel. "We no longer care if you're a little bit late." Rachel slips into her seat.

"I've made trouble for the Nazis," she whispers to Max.

"Children can't do that," he answers.

"They can, too. The Eternal Jew is blind. I'll show you on our way home."

"Crazy kid," Max says. "Girls are always saying things that can't possibly be true."

❖   *Brother John*

"Are you sleeping, are you sleeping, Brother John, Brother John?"

"Join in, Riwkah!" Mr. Noach calls out. "Pay attention, girl!"

Rachel, Lex, and Riwkah have already tried many times to sing "Brother John" in a round. Singing in unison isn't that hard to do, but singing a song in a round can be very difficult.

"I want your parents to be proud of your singing. That is why you must practice hard for tomorrow evening."

"Yes, Mr. Noach," the three said at the same time.

Tomorrow at the parents' night Rachel will be singing "Brother John" with Lex and Riwkah. "You always do everything together," Mr. Noach said. "Now you may sing together, too. Go practice in the teachers' room. When you've learned the song, come back to the class. We'll listen to you then."

It goes very well! They laughed and laughed because Riwkah kept coming in too early, but now everything is quite all right.

"Come in. We'll listen to you now." Mr. Noach turns to the class. "Quiet, children! Rachel and Riwkah and Lex are going to sing for us." He taps a stick on the table nearest to him. "Quiet! Here comes the trio 'RiLeRa.' Riwkah, Lex, and Rachel."

"Are you sleeping, are you sleeping, Brother John . . ." They sing very well. No one makes a mistake.

"Wonderful! Applause!" Mr. Noach calls. "Tomorrow morning you can practice again and then I don't want you to sing anymore until tomorrow evening. Otherwise it's too much. And now you are dismissed, children. Tomorrow is another day."

"Today we're not going to begin with our lessons right away," Mr. Noach announces at school the next morning.

"Something terrible has happened. Last night a number of children were taken away by the Germans."

The class is very quiet. The children look at one another.

"You weren't taken away," Benny says to Rachel.

"No, and you weren't taken away, either, were you?" Rachel says to Benny. She looks around her. Riwkah is there, but Lex's seat is empty.

"How are we going to sing tonight?" Rachel asks the teacher.

"Be brave," answers Mr. Noach. "Jews keep going, children, as long as they can. Tonight we're going to listen to the duo RiRa and they will sing 'Brother John' for us."

❖ *Going into Hiding*

"This is Mrs. Helsloot," says Mother. "She has come to take you. You are going into hiding."

"Going into hiding?" Rachel doesn't know what her mother means. "I'm not going with her," she replies.

"My dear, you must."

"Why haven't Papa and you told us? And what does 'going into hiding' mean?" Rachel asks.

"Going into hiding is this: you hide from the Germans," her mother explains. "It is becoming too dangerous to wait here at home until they come get us. Go along. Esther and you will sleep one night at Mrs. Helsloot's. Tomorrow she will bring you to a village nearby. Papa and I will be there, too. Come, dear, get your scooter and go along." Mother says it in such a special way that Rachel has to listen.

"Remember your scooter," says Mrs. Helsloot. "It is for Anke. You can't use it for the time being, anyway."

"Who is Anke?" asks Rachel.

"She is my little daughter. You'll see her when we're home," Mrs. Helsloot answers.

"Where are we going?" asks Esther.

"I can't tell you," says Mrs. Helsloot. "Imagine that the Germans should arrest us and ask you where you're going. It really is better that you don't know."

Rachel doesn't understand a single thing that Mrs. Helsloot says. After all, it has happened so suddenly.

"Go now." Mother gives Rachel a kiss. "I'll give your love to Papa later. Tomorrow we'll see each other again."

Rachel kisses her mother and they go. She and Esther are on the scooter, and Mrs. Helsloot is walking next to them.

A German flag is hanging from the house on the corner. Under the flag two children are busily eating. It is Lotte and Elly. They are celebrating Hitler's birthday.

"Tomorrow is Hitler's birthday," Lotte said yesterday. "We are going to eat delicious cakes and you're not getting any."

"Keep going! Don't look back!" calls Mrs. Helsloot.

After ten minutes they are walking in a street where they have never been before. "Stand still. Something important is going to happen now," says Mrs. Helsloot.

The woman reaches into her coat pocket. She takes out a scissors and goes toward Esther and Rachel with it.

Rachel feels her star being pulled. She feels Mrs. Helsloot cutting threads. "Don't!" she cries out. "We're not allowed to walk outside without a star. We'll be picked up then." She wants to stop Mrs. Helsloot, but the woman is holding her hand.

"Rachel," Mrs. Helsloot informs her, "from now on you must do what I say, at least if you don't want to be picked up. You're not allowed to walk about *with* a star now."

Mrs. Helsloot continues cutting. With one more pull she has the yellow patch in her hand. They are standing by a sewer. The star disappears into it. Now it is Esther's turn. Esther doesn't mind it so much. Quietly she lets Mrs. Helsloot go about her work.

"Come, children, we'll go on."

The girls step on the scooter again. Esther is standing in front, Rachel in back.

"Goodness!" exclaims Mrs. Helsloot, and she puts a hand over her mouth. "Look at that, Rachel!" The woman points to her coat, where the star was. "You can see exactly where that rotten star was. The rest of your coat is lighter blue than the place where your star was. Esther, make sure that your head remains in front of Rachel's chest."

Rachel is terrified. Her hands are sweaty and her heart is beating in her throat. She wants to go home to Papa and Mama. She does *not* want to go into hiding at all. Imagine that some Germans should come and see that blue patch.

"Heinz," one German would say to another. "This child has taken off her star, and that's not allowed. We'll arrest her."

After they have been walking for fifteen minutes, Mrs. Helsloot says: "Here we are. Go inside quickly."

They come into a house where three girls and a man are sitting at a table. "This is my husband and these are my children," Mrs. Helsloot says.

"Hello, Mr. Helsloot." Rachel and Esther shake hands with Mrs. Helsloot's husband.

"Take your coat off," says the man. "My God, Tine, how did you dare to walk so with that child? She has a star on, a blue one."

"I know that," Mrs. Helsloot explains to her husband. "Luckily it went all right. I'll try to bleach that blue star this evening. I'll get that imprint out."

"I hope so," says Mr. Helsloot. He turns to Rachel and Esther. "Would you like a sandwich? Mmm, a hearty sandwich with brown bread and bacon." Bacon? Rachel is already becoming sick just hearing the word bacon. Doesn't that man know that Jewish children may not eat bacon?

"Pardon me," Mr. Helsloot apologizes. "I hadn't thought about it. You don't eat pork."

In the evening Mrs. Helsloot brings them to bed. "Sleep tight," she says. "Tomorrow I'll take you to your parents. We'll go on the tram to Delft, and what happens after that you'll see for yourself."

"We haven't been *allowed* to take a tram for a long time," Rachel wants to say, but she sighs and holds her tongue. She is terribly tired from everything.

"I'm going to try to bleach your coat now. Then when we go tomorrow you'll have no star on it — no yellow one and no blue one. Good night."

Each girl receives a kiss from Mrs. Helsloot. "That's nice," Rachel thinks.

The sisters crawl close to each other. It is pleasant to be together in one bed. At home they sleep in separate beds.

"Where are we now?" whispers Esther.

"Wait," Rachel whispers back. "I'll look." Very quietly she gets out of bed. She opens the curtain. On the other side of the street is a little sign with a street name on it. "All . . . ar . . . I can't read it very well."

"Wait, I'll turn the light on," says Esther, and she pulls the little string hanging above the bed.

"Don't! You must never do that again. When you're in hiding you must never turn the light on when the curtains are open. And the curtains — those must never, never be open, for no one must see you!"

Mrs. Helsloot is standing in the room. "You just have to get used to it," she continues. "It will be hard. Don't be so foolish anymore, all right?"

"No, Mrs. Helsloot," the girls say at the same time.

"It is difficult with your coat, but it probably will work," Mrs. Helsloot says.

"And if it doesn't?" Rachel asks her.

"Then you'll have to put that coat on, anyway," the woman tells her. "You'll just hold a book in the place where your star was."

Rachel can't sleep. Esther is breathing very quietly next to her. She is sleeping.

Rachel thinks about tomorrow. Perhaps she will have to go outside without a star and yet with a star. How difficult everything is today.

The door opens very softly.

Mrs. Helsloot is standing in front of the bed. "It worked," she whispers. "No one can see that you have had a star on your coat. Sleep well. Good night."

"Good night, Mrs. Helsloot." Rachel sighs. "And give my regards to your husband."

❖   *They Aren't Any Different*

The second night in hiding is past.

How happy Rachel and Esther were yesterday when they saw their father and mother again. They find it comforting to sleep near their own parents, even if they aren't at home but in a strange house, in a rectory in Schipluiden.

Mrs. Helsloot brought them there. "This is Father Thijssen," she said to the girls. "Shake hands with him."

"Hello, sir," they said to a man in a black robe with a whole lot of buttons on it.

"Hello, children. Welcome to Schipluiden. Your parents are upstairs," Father Thijssen told them.

The Hartogs are all sitting at the table now. "Dora, my housekeeper, and Neeltje, my servant girl, will bring you your breakfast," the priest said when he came to see them very early this morning. "They weren't here when you arrived yesterday. They had the day off, but now you can get acquainted with each other."

"It's just like being on vacation," Mother exclaims. "I don't have to make our own breakfast."

Someone knocks loudly on the door. "Come in," calls Father.

The sound of laughter fills the hall. "You first," Rachel hears. "No, you first. Don't be so silly."

"Come in!" Father calls out again.

"Go on!" Rachel hears.

The door bursts open. Two women enter in single file. One carries a tray while the other has a teapot in her hand. They remain standing in the room.

"Put the teapot down, Neel," says the woman with the tray. Neel does as she is told and sets the teapot on the table. She gazes intently at Father; then she looks at Mother.

"Dora," she exclaims, "they aren't any different."

"You see," Dora explains, "we've never seen Jews before. That's why it took a while before we dared to come in."

Neeltje runs out of the room. "Enjoy your breakfast," Dora calls, and she runs after Neeltje.

❖ Candy

The Hartogs have been at the rectory for seven weeks now, and they have never yet been downstairs to the room where Father Thijssen lives.

"Too dangerous," the priest says. "Do you see that iron tower in the pasture there? Every now and then the Nazis climb it to view the surrounding area. Perhaps they can look inside here. It's better for you to remain safe and sound upstairs."

"When Father Thijssen and Dora are at church, we'll sneak downstairs," Rachel has promised Esther. That is easy to say, for the priest and his housekeeper have never gone to church together. Until this morning. It is unusually quiet downstairs. Normally Rachel can hear Dora rattling the pots and plates around, or she hears Father Thijssen singing, but there is only silence now.

Father and Mother are reading. She and Esther are playing a game.

"Six," calls Esther, who is about to move a red pawn.

"Esther, we're going," Rachel whispers.

"Where are you going?" asks Mother.

"We're going to walk a little bit in the hall."

"All right, but quietly, okay?"

"Yes, Mama."

The girls tiptoe out of the room. They are now used to the fact that they are not allowed to make any noise. When they first went into hiding, being quiet had been very difficult for them.

They are now at the stairs. Carefully, Rachel sets her foot on the step. "Come on, Esther," she whispers.

It is going well. They are almost downstairs now. One more step and then . . .

At the foot of the stairs lies Timmie, Father Thijssen's dog. He is on a chain, for he is a watchdog. Timmie is nice, but it seems as if he has become a mad dog now. He rattles his chain and jumps up on Esther. He growls and bares his teeth.

"Rotten dog!" Esther calls out. "Horrible dog. In all these seven weeks we've never been downstairs and because of you we can't go now. We want some adventure!"

They have to go back, for they don't dare walk past the dog. Their adventure has failed.

"Don't go back into the room," Rachel whispers. "Come with me, I have an idea. Mama has a box of candy in her suitcase. If we give Timmie the candy, we'll be able to get through."

They walk to the hall closet. There is Mother's suitcase. The girls grope among the blouses and the slips until they find the candy.

* * *

"What are you doing in my suitcase?" Mother is standing in the hall.

"Nothing, we're so bored," Rachel answers. "We want to know what you have in it."

"It's *my* suitcase. If you go snooping through it then I don't have anything left to call my own. How difficult you both are today. If we weren't in hiding I would punish you. Say, did you hear Timmie barking? What could be the matter with him?"

Startled, the girls look at each other.

"I don't know, Mama," answers Esther.

"I don't know, either," Rachel says.

She has the box of candy hidden in the pocket of her dress. "We'll go again, Esther," she whispers.

They walk down the stairs very quietly. When they have almost reached Timmie Rachel calls, "Good dog. Come! Come on, we have candy for you."

Timmie approaches the children. Rachel takes a handful of candy from the box and lets him sniff it; all the candy disappears with one lick of his long, pink tongue. Then he lies calmly down. He drags the chain over the stone floor for a bit, but then there is silence.

They walk through the hall. "Here is where the room must be," Rachel whispers. "Come on." She opens the door to a large room.

"What a pretty chair!" Esther calls out. She runs inside and lets herself fall into a big chair. She jumps up and lets herself fall again; the harder she falls, the higher she bounces back up.

"Don't do that. You'll break the chair."

They walk through the room. The door to the kitchen is open; the girls peek inside.

"Nice pans, aren't they?" Esther exclaims.

"I'll say!"

"Let's go into the garden," says Esther. "I want to see everything that's down here."

Rachel is frightened. "Nothing doing, we're going back upstairs."

"I want to go into the garden."

"Do you see that iron tower?" Rachel whispers. "There's a big fat Nazi with a telescope up there, and he's looking at you. Yes, he's looking at you!"

"No, really?" Esther is almost in tears.

"I'm only joking," Rachel tells her, "but what we're doing now is dangerous. Father Thijssen told me so himself."

"Let's get out of here," says Esther.

Timmie is still lying peacefully asleep in front of the steps. They must step over him to go upstairs. When the girls are on the third step, the chain begins to rattle. Timmie stands up on his four feet and begins to bark very loudly.

"Quiet!" Rachel calls, but it is too late. At the top of the stairs is their mother.

"What are you doing there?"

"We went downstairs for a little while."

"Come up here at once. You both know that you're not allowed downstairs. I'm very angry with you."

"We were so curious and we were so bored," says Esther.

"That doesn't matter," Mother answers. "Do you want the Nazis to get you?"

"Yes, we do!" Esther calls out. "Then at least we'd be able to go outside!"

❖ *Prayer*

Before Rachel goes to sleep, she says a little prayer.

She finds it wonderful to talk to God. Rachel tells Him everything that happened during the past day. That isn't really necessary, because God knows everything, but to whom else is she to tell her experiences, then?

"In God's name I lay me down to sleep to arise again early tomorrow in good health. *Amen sela.*"

Rachel doesn't know what that last part means. It is Hebrew and it sounds pretty.

Rachel never used to pray at home, but Mama has now taught her how, and she is glad to be doing it. Rachel herself has made up something to add to the prayer.

"God, please save the people in Vught, Westerbork, and Poland." When Rachel says these words, she shuts her eyes very tightly. She clasps her hands together very hard. God *must* listen.

"God, save Grandpa, Grandma, Uncle Jacob, Marga, Mientje, Riwkah, Herman, Johnny, Uncle Maurits, and Aunt Malli."

Rachel can keep going like this for hours, for there are so many people in the concentration camps at Vught, Westerbork, and Poland. She keeps going until Uncle Maurits, Aunt Malli, and Johnny. Otherwise it becomes too many.

Rachel is tired this evening. She spent the entire day reading. You become bleary-eyed from that. She is lying in bed.

"God, save Grandpa, Grandma, Uncle Jacob, Marga, Riwkah, Herman . . . God, I can't pray anymore."

When the Hartogs are sitting at the breakfast table the next morning, Father Thijssen comes upstairs. "Here, a card for you," he says. "There is a German postmark on it. I received it through the underground."

He gives the card to Mother. She reads it. Her hands begin to tremble. "My God, Malli and Johnny and

Maurits have been sent from Westerbork to Poland. Here, a farewell card."

When Rachel lies in bed in the evening she prays:
"Dear God. Yesterday I forgot to ask.
"Dear God, save Aunt Malli and Uncle Maurits and Johnny.
"Save Aunt Malli and Uncle Maurits and Johnny.
"Please, God, save Aunt Malli and Uncle Maurits and Johnny.
"Is that all right, God?"

❖ *Standing Watch*

The time has come. Today Rachel must go stand in front of the window to see if there is any danger. Hans, who is in the underground, has come up with the idea.

"People," he said, "people, we have to make a plan. If the Nazis should ever find out our address, we're not going to just turn ourselves in." Hans said "our address" because now and then he hides in the rectory, too.

"Hans must disappear for a while. He's made trouble

for the Nazis again," Father says then, but Rachel doesn't know what he means.

Hans has devised the "lookout plan." They have to take turns standing watch at the window in the front room. Anyone who sees something suspicious must immediately blow a whistle to warn the others. Then, with the person standing watch bringing up the rear, they must run up to the attic, out through the roof window, and then sit on the ladder that leans against the sloping roof. Each person has his own place on the roof, high above the countryside. In order for them to be able to climb through the window, a ladder is set up in the attic, day and night.

"Remember," says Hans at each practice drill, "whoever is the last person must kick the attic ladder away, otherwise the Germans will see that we've climbed out the window."

They practice often. When the whistle blows they must clear everything away quickly. There cannot be a single cup left lying around or a single book, either. There must not be a single trace left behind them, for everyone has to believe that only Father Thijssen and Dora live in the rectory.

Rachel gets a terrible stomachache at each practice session; it is so bad that she becomes nauseated from the pain. She doesn't tell anyone about it, for no one can help her. Each person is much too busy trying to escape to the roof.

* * *

Rachel is now standing in front of the big window in the "Mary Room." She has given the room this name because there is a statue of Mary in it.

"Holy Mary," says Father Thijssen. Rachel says only "Mary," for Jewish children don't consider Mary to be holy.

If the Nazis should come, she would have to blow the whistle loudly. Very loudly! But what if she doesn't see them in time? What if she can't warn the others in time? Then a Nazi would grab her by the neck and shout, "Ha, I have the first Jew. There's sure to be more of them!"

"Holy Mary, please don't let them come, please don't!" Rachel looks at the statue. The statue is silent, but it is smiling. Is it smiling at her, perhaps?

Rachel jumps when the door opens. It is her mother, who has come to bring her a cup of tea.

"So, my big girl, how's it going? Shall I stay with you a little while?"

"You don't have to. I'm not bored," Rachel answers.

"Another half hour, Rachel. Then I'll take over for you."

Mother disappears. Rachel hears her footsteps in the hall.

The church clock chimes above her head. "Another half hour, Mary," she tells the statue. "Do you hear the church clock? Another half hour."

Rachel looks across the canal that runs beside the rectory. On the other side of the water is a farm. People are drinking tea over there, just as she is. A whole family is seated around a large table. The people are talking; Rachel can see that by the gesturing of their hands.

She looks from the canal to the road, from the road to the canal. A horse is walking past, pulling a cart behind it. Rachel can hear the click-clacking of the hooves and the squeaking of the wheels. After the horse and wagon have passed by, the road is empty.

Empty? If Rachel looks very carefully she can see something in the distance. She must be dreaming. It isn't true. That green auto there, fully loaded with men wearing helmets, can't be a Nazi van — or can it?

"Holy Mary, it's not true, is it?"

It *is* true. The van comes closer. The men who are bulging out of the windows are pointing at her.

Rachel hears the sound of a whistle. She feels her legs carrying her up to the attic. Everyone else has disappeared through the window of the roof; now it is her turn to go. She climbs the ladder standing in the attic. When the upper part of her body is hanging in the window opening, she kicks the ladder away. It falls on the wooden floor with a crash. Rachel closes the window, then breathlessly goes to sit against the slanted roof.

It is too late! She blew the whistle too late. She wants to scream, "Take us, here we are!" but not a sound comes out of her mouth. Soon the window will open and a man in a helmet will appear. Rachel will be the first to be captured, for the person standing watch sits closest to the window.

Look, it is happening already! The window opens very slowly. A blond head appears. "Don't worry," says the voice coming from the head. "It's safe."

It is Father Thijssen coming to get them off the roof, not one of the Nazis she saw when she was standing watch.

Rachel is the first one off the roof. "Well done, my girl," the priest commends her. "You blew the whistle right on time. But they didn't come for you."

"They were all pointing at me!"

"No, do you know what they were pointing at? At the orange flowers in the garden. Do you know that the last name of our queen, who is in England now, is Orange? That's why the Dutch people are not allowed to have orange flowers in their gardens."

When Hans tells Rachel later in the day that he is proud of her, she bursts into tears.

"You don't have to do it anymore," Hans comforts her. "Maybe you're still a little too young to be able to stand watch."

❖ *They Have Just Left*

Father Thijssen opens the door with a tug. "People," he says, "I have something to tell you. You're going to have to leave."

"No, not really?" Mother asks.

"Yes, I'm sorry to say," answers the priest. "Something is going to happen now that hasn't happened in thirty years. A chaplain has been appointed, and he'll have to live in your room. He'll be coming in ten days."

"A chaplain? What's that?" asks Esther.

"A chaplain, Esther, is someone who helps the priest, an assistant," Father Thijssen explains to her.

"Where are we to go?" Father asks, with a sigh. "We'll have to alert the underground."

"Believe me, throughout my whole life I've seen things happen that sometimes don't make any sense to you, yet what does happen always seems to happen for the best. God has a reason for everything He does," says the priest.

"I'm going to give myself up to the Germans," Father says. "I've had enough. We have to keep finding places to hide, again and again. I can't take it anymore."

"We're not going to turn ourselves in, David. We can't do that to our children. Think about what Father Thijssen said." Mother tries to reason with Father.

"It's nonsense," Father answers. "I'm not a Catholic. I don't believe in fate."

"Tomorrow we'll find a solution," Rachel says all of a sudden. She doesn't know why she said it; she had to, that's all.

"Rachel, you're a Miss Know-It-All," Mother exclaims. "You're like a fortune teller at a carnival."

But it turns out to be true. Hans comes over the next day to report that he has found an address for them.

"Can you tell us where?" Mother asks.

"I'd rather not tell you until next week," answers Hans.

The Hartogs are now walking in the garden of the rectory together with Hans, who will take them to their new address. They have not been outside for seven months. Rachel would like to look at the sky, at the stars, but she is becoming so dizzy that she must take hold of Mother's hand.

"How pretty the stars are," she exclaims. "And how wonderful it smells outside."

"Hurry up, Rachel. Don't talk so much," says Hans. "Quickly, get into that car over there."

Father Thijssen has been walking along with them. He is still standing there as the automobile begins to drive away. He waves with both hands. "God bless you!" he shouts.

"God bless you!" Mother replies.

"Where are we going?" asks Esther.

"We're going north," Hans answers. "I can't tell you more than that."

After they have been riding for about an hour, Hans says, "We're almost there."

They drive into a city. The houses look old and there is a lot of water all around them. "This is Hoorn," Hans explains. "And there is your next hiding place." He stops in front of a house situated on a long street. "Come on," he calls. "The address is number thirteen."

Hans rings the doorbell. A woman opens the door. "I'm Aunt Annie," she says, introducing herself. "And this is Uncle Jan." She points to a man who is standing in the hall.

"Pleased to meet you," say Father and Mother.

Not at all pleased to meet you, thinks Rachel.

"Let's go upstairs. I'll show you where your room is." Aunt Annie is already on the steps.

The Hartogs follow her. "Come in. Here it is," Aunt Annie announces.

"Where do we sleep?" asks Mother. "I don't see a bed anywhere."

"When we aren't hiding any other people, you may sleep in the folding bed here in the room," Aunt Annie explains. "The children will get a double bed in the hall."

"Thank you," says Mother.

"I'll stay with you tonight," says Hans. "I'd like to go to bed now, for I have to get up early tomorrow."

"We're going to bed, too, and the children as well." Father yawns. "I'll go set up the folding bed."

Rachel and Esther are lying together in a bed in the hall. After a while Hans crawls in next to them.

Father and Mother come in to kiss the girls good night. Mother kisses Hans, too. "Thank you, Hans," she whispers. "You do so much for us."

"It's nothing," he answers sleepily.

In the middle of the night the telephone begins to ring. Aunt Annie is already standing in the corridor.

"Wait." Hans holds her back. "I'll go downstairs."

He runs down the steps. Rachel can hear his voice from upstairs. He must have left the door open.

"How awful," she hears. "Have they taken him away?" Rachel sits up in bed. Whom have they taken away? Won't it ever stop? She hears Hans slowly coming up the steps.

"Tell us," says Aunt Annie.

"The telephone call was from someone in the underground." Hans looks at Aunt Annie, then at Rachel. "They came to the rectory to arrest David and Ruth and the children. One German and two Dutchmen turned the whole place upside down. 'You're out of luck, the family has just left,' Father Thijssen said, and then they took him away."

"How does the underground know that?" Aunt Annie looks wide-eyed at Hans.

"They heard about it from Dora, the housekeeper."

Father and Mother are now in the hall, too. "They've arrested Father Thijssen," Rachel tells them.

"Rachel, that can't be, you're fibbing," says Mother. "We spoke with him only this evening."

"It's unbelievable, but it's true," says Hans.

"God bless Father Thijssen." Mother weeps.

"Dirty rotten Nazis!" shouts Father. "Dirty rotten traitors!"

❖ *More People*

"Today more people will be coming to hide here," Aunt Annie informs them.

"It will make things pretty crowded," Father says. "Who will be coming?"

"I can't tell you. It's a surprise."

"A surprise? How can that be? What kind of surprise?" Rachel asks. She is terribly curious.

"They're sure to be unpleasant people," Mother complains. "And where are we all to sleep? We only have two beds."

"Downstairs is a sofa where you and David can sleep. We don't have much room as it is," replies Aunt Annie a bit angrily.

"If the people are unpleasant, I'm not going to talk to them. I have enough books to read. I don't like to be with so many strangers in such a small space," Mother grumbles.

There is a knock on the door. "Come in!" calls Mother. A woman enters the room. She is small and she has blue eyes. Rachel cannot see the rest of her, for she has a scarf tied around her face. It certainly must be cold outside.

A man comes into the room, too, but this is someone Rachel recognizes. "Grandpa!" she shouts.

"Pa!" screams Mother.

"Children!" the woman calls out, and she removes the scarf from her face. "Children, we haven't seen each other for a whole year, and now . . . suddenly . . ."

"Hello." There is another person standing in the room, a woman. "Hello, children. My name is Trijn. My real name is Clara, but Trijn is my name while I'm in hiding. I've come to hide with you, too, together with your grandparents."

"More can come. More can come," Mother sings. "How happy I am."

"Let's sit down," suggests Father. "It will be pretty crowded in here. Where have you been until now?"

"We can't tell you," answers Grandpa. "Let's not ask each other too many questions. Later, when the war is over."

They are sitting silently around the table. They keep looking at one another; it has been such a long time since they were together.

Aunt Annie comes into the room. "How nice and quiet you are," she comments. "It's better than I expected with seven people.

"I shall divide up the beds now," she continues. "Trijn and the children can have the bed in the hall. Grandpa and Grandma will have the folding bed, and Ruth and David can sleep on the sofa. We'll have to make do with what we have, for we don't have any other choice."

"That doesn't matter," exclaims Mother. "I'm so happy to see my parents again."

"I'm jealous of you," says Father.

"After the war you'll see your parents again," Mother comforts him.

"Let's hope so," Father answers.

"Practice it one more time," says Mother. "What is your name now?"

"Rachel Hartog" is what she almost says, but that isn't allowed. Rachel Hartog no longer exists. Rachel Hartog has been rechristened Ria van Willigen.

"Away with your Jewish names," Aunt Annie told them. "From now on your last name is van Willigen and your first names are: Jan Willem." She points to Father.

"Janny." Her pointing finger moves toward Mother.

"Maaike." It is Esther's turn.

"Ria."

Rachel has a difficult time getting used to everyone calling her Ria. She often says "Hello, Rachel" to herself, for she is afraid that she will forget what her real name is. She often says "Hello, Ria van Willigen" to herself, too, for if she should be caught she must immediately be able to say, "I'm Ria van Willigen and my address is Haantje ninety-six in Gorkum."

Rachel hates the name Ria. When the war is over she is going to throw that Ria right out the window! And she will never call Esther Maaike again. Never!

Tomorrow is Rachel's birthday. She will be twelve years old. She has seen a package in the closet, a flat, purple package, and she is certain it is a birthday gift. Perhaps it is a book. That would be lovely, for she has read the book that she brought with her from home one hundred times already.

"Happy birthday, Ria," her mother says the next morning. "And many more years of health and peace."

"Happy birthday, Ria. Here is a present for you." Father gives her the package that she has seen lying in the closet.

Rachel receives gifts from everyone; a little box of handkerchiefs from Grandpa and Grandma, a bottle of nail polish from Aunt Trijn, and a pencil from Esther. "Thank you, everybody. How happy I am with all these presents," Rachel says.

"Aren't you going to open our package, Ria?" asks her father.

"Of course I am. I wanted to wait and build up my curiosity." Rachel opens the purple package very carefully. A splendid poetry album appears out of the wrapping.

"How pretty," Rachel says. "It looks like an album of mine that I had to leave at home. That's wonderful, now I have one again. Will you all write a verse in my new album?"

"I can't write," says Esther.

"I'll help you, Maaike," Father promises.

"I'm going to polish my nails and I'm going to blow my nose. What a lot of presents I've gotten!" exclaims Rachel.

"Are you happy, Rachel?" asks Esther.

"You have to say 'Are you happy, Ria,'" Father admonishes her.

"Oh, that's right. Are you happy, Ria?"

"Yes."

The festivities are over now. Everyone is sitting very quietly; they have to, for the cleaning woman will be coming soon, and she isn't supposed to know that so many people are hidden upstairs. They can't even talk anymore.

Rachel is sitting at the table with the poetry album before her. She wants to write the first poem on the first page herself. She takes the pencil Esther gave her and writes:

> This album is mine
> As long as I hope to abide.
> Rachel is the name
> My parents gave to me.
> Hartog is my last name,
> It's from my father's side.
> Groningen is my birthplace . . .

"Ria, for God's sake, what are you doing? Stop it!" Mother is standing behind her. She snatches the album and begins to tear the first page out.

"Don't, Mama!" Rachel cries out. "Don't tear it!" Mother keeps on tearing. "Stop, Mama!" Rachel begins to hit Mama on the head with her fists. She is shouting, she is crying. She never, ever wants to be quiet again.

Rachel feels Mother pulling her into her lap. She feels her mother kissing her and whispering soothing words into her ear.

"Child, child, what do you want?" her mother asks.

"Nothing," she sobs. "Nothing, I just want to be Rachel Hartog."

❖ *Smiling*

"Come on," says Aunt Annie. "Come downstairs with me. I want to take a photograph of you."

"Of us?" Father asks.

"No, of the girls," Annie says, and turns to the children. "If you should be caught, I would want something to remember you by. That is why I want to take the picture."

Rachel finds it wonderful, for she can go downstairs now. Occasionally she goes downstairs in the evening, but never during the daytime.

When they get downstairs Aunt Annie opens the door

leading out to the garden. Rachel runs back into the hallway. Esther follows her.

"What are you doing now? Come on, I want to take your picture. Get outside!"

"Outside? I don't want to go outside. It's so light, the neighbors might see us," Rachel protests.

"It won't take long." Aunt Annie gives her a push.

They are standing outside. Aunt Annie has spread a white sheet over the fence that separates her yard from the neighbors'. "It will make the photo turn out prettier," she tells them. "Go sit down over there, in front of the sheet." She places the girls on a little bench, then stands before them with a camera. "Smile!"

Esther begins to laugh very loudly.

"Without any noise. Smile quietly!" commands Aunt Annie.

Rachel does her best to smile and to sit still, but she cannot. She is very frightened; they have been kept in Aunt Annie's and Uncle Jan's attic room for three long months. That is why it feels so eerie to be outside now.

"Don't look so sour. You're twelve years old already. You know how to smile by now, don't you?" Aunt Annie spreads her lips apart, tilts her head back a little, and reveals her large, white teeth.

Rachel tries to imitate Annie, but the woman is not satisfied. "Never mind," Aunt Annie grumbles.

"Prrt," goes the camera. The photograph has been

taken. "Stupid," says Aunt Annie. "You can't even smile."
She brings the girls back upstairs.

"Well, did the photo turn out pretty?" asks Father.

"No," says Aunt Annie in disgust and points to
Rachel. "That big, stupid one didn't want to smile."

❖   *Pietje Prays*

"Oh, God, isn't that sweet," exclaims Aunt Trijn. "Do
you know what Pietje's foster mother writes?" She waves
the letter that she has just read. "Pietje can pray so beautifully. He can even cross himself."

Pietje is five years old. His real name is Eli, and he is
Aunt Trijn's little son.

"You think that's sweet!" says Grandpa, a little too
loudly. "Do you think that's sweet? They take our children and our prayers away from us."

"What difference does it make? As long as my child
has it good he may pray however he wants."

"Fine, have it your way. We won't discuss it any further."

Pietje is now sitting with them up in the attic room. Joke,
his foster mother, wants very much to show him to his
own mother.

"Will you come sit in my lap?" Aunt Trijn asks, and stretches her arms out toward him.

"No," Pietje answers. "I'll stay with me mother." He leans his head against Joke's breast.

"He talks differently than he used to," Aunt Trijn remarks.

"Yes, nice, isn't it? And oh, can he pray. Let's hear you, Pietje."

Pietje crosses himself. "In the name of the Father and the Son and the Holy Ghost." Grandpa turns his back to the child. Pietje continues. "Hail Mary. Uh, uh . . ."

"Come on," says Joke. "Think, you know it."

Pietje looks up at Aunt Trijn from above his folded hands. He sighs deeply. "Full of mercy. *Baruch ata, Adonai Eloheinu, melech haolam . . .*"

Grandpa turns around with a jerk. Tears are streaming down his cheeks. "*Shema Yisraeil: Adonai Eloheinu, Adonai echad.* Hear, O Israel: the Lord is our God, the Lord is One." Grandpa sings the age-old Jewish prayer very softly. The others sing very softly with him.

Pietje lies on Joke's breast with his thumb half out of his mouth. He is sleeping.

❖ Scarlet Fever

Aunt Annie has hung a large sign on her door. QUARAN-TINE: SCARLET FEVER is written upon it in Dutch and in German. "The Nazis won't dare come in now. They're scared to death of scarlet fever," says Aunt Annie, satis-fied.

Rachel has ten thousand spots over her whole body. She has a sore throat and fever. She is very sick, yet she is happy, too. She has been living in constant fear of the Nazis for such a long time now. Perhaps Aunt Annie can leave the sign on the door for the rest of the war. Then Rachel would never be caught, and she would never have to be afraid, either.

Mama sits at her bedside the whole day and sings the old songs that she learned from *her* grandmother. There is a lullaby that Rachel could keep listening to forever:

> My child, my child,
> You must go to sleep.
> The stars are shining
> In the sky,
> And mother is by your side.
> Sleep, my little child, sleep tight.

This little song is soothing to her. It makes it seem as if Mama really can protect her from the Nazis.

Rachel lies in Aunt Annie's bed instead of in the bed in the hallway, where she usually sleeps. "You need rest when you're this sick. You may have my bed," Aunt Annie said.

Red spots are not bad. A sore throat is not bad.

Fever is wonderful. Scarlet fever is wonderful.

Perhaps Rachel will be sick for the rest of the war!

❖ *Breasts*

Rachel runs her hands very gently along the upper part of her body. It really is true. Her breasts are beginning to develop.

First the left side began to hurt a little, and now the right side is beginning to hurt a bit, too. Rachel didn't know that getting breasts would be painful, but she doesn't mind it at all. She is rather proud, for she is truly growing up now. Yesterday she removed the pockets from her knitted dress; when those ridiculous pockets were covering her chest, no one could see her breasts and everyone should see them because they are so pretty.

Gerrit, who is in the underground, will be coming this

evening. He has been over a couple of times before, and Rachel thinks he is nice. Gerrit will have to see her breasts, but how is she to show them to him? She can't take her clothes off and say, "Look, Gerrit, my breasts are growing." She can't do that.

If Rachel were not in hiding, she would be able to discuss the matter with a friend, and in gym class all the girls would be able to see for themselves that Rachel is growing up. There is no one to see her breasts here; that is why Gerrit *must* look.

"Go to bed, children," says Mother.

"I don't want to. I want to wait for Gerrit," Rachel protests.

"Gerrit will be coming late, you know that. Hup, pajamas on and to bed with you."

There is nothing to be done. You have to listen to your mother even if you are in hiding. Grumbling she goes to bed.

"I don't feel like telling any stories," she says to Esther.

"Silly," Esther replies, "I'll tell one then. Once upon a time there was . . . ."

"Shut up, I'm tired."

Rachel can't sleep. She keeps thinking about her breasts. It seems like they are getting bigger by the minute. How warm she is. She takes her pajama top off. She is stifling hot.

The doorbell rings very loudly. Usually Rachel is frightened when that happens, but tonight she knows it is Gerrit. She throws her bed covers off so that her bare chest will be clearly visible to him.

"Hello, little maid," Gerrit whispers as he stands by her bed. "How are you?"

"Fine." Rachel sits up so that he can have a better look at her breasts.

"Put your pajama top on," he says. "You'll catch cold."

"Don't you see anything, Gerrit?"

"No, what am I supposed to see?"

"My breasts are getting big."

Gerrit begins to roar with laughter. "Oh, that's funny. Two little peas on a board and you call them breasts. Good night, little maid."

Rachel is furious. That rotten Gerrit! She doesn't need him, even if he *is* in the underground. Perhaps he will be captured by the Nazis. It would serve him right!

❖ *Mr. Pear*

One day a strange man comes into the room. He reaches his hand out toward Father. "My name is Pear," he says.

"My name is Apple," jokes Father.

How weird they're acting, Rachel thinks. "If you have a secret name, why pick one that is so unusual?"

"We've come to fetch your daughters," says Mr. Pear. "We of the underground have gotten word that it is no longer safe for them here."

Rachel sees that her father has become as white as a sheet. Mother is sitting in a chair with her hands over her eyes.

"We'll go with them," says Father. "We won't let our children go alone."

"We don't have an address for adults yet. I'll come back to get you and your wife in a couple of days."

"Will you take us to our children then?" Father asks.

"No, you'll go somewhere else, to other people."

"Where are *we* to go?" asks Grandpa.

"We still haven't found accommodations for you and your wife."

"You haven't found a place for me, either, have you?" Aunt Trijn looks very frightened.

"Unfortunately we haven't, but we'll keep looking."

Esther and Rachel are ready to leave. Mother is packing a bag with their things. Rachel keeps her book under her arm; she wants to have that close to her always.

"Where are they going?" Mother asks Mr. Pear.

"They're going to a village here in the area. They'll be living with nice people who have no children of their own. We'll leave when it's dark outside," Mr. Pear says.

They are sitting together very quietly. Rachel is in Mother's lap, Esther in Father's. Grandpa, Grandma, and Aunt Trijn are sitting with them, too.

"Ria, come with me to the hallway," says her mother. "I have something to discuss with you."

They enter the corridor. "Come, let's sit together here on the bed," Mother says. "You are the oldest," she continues. "Take good care of Maaike and do exactly what the new people tell you to."

"Yes, Mama."

When they return to the room, everyone is still sitting in the same place. "Dear God, let it stay light outside," Rachel asks silently.

"Come on, let's go," Mr. Pear announces as he rises from his seat. "It's almost dark." How terribly big Mr. Pear is, now that he is standing!

Rachel takes Esther's hand. "Say goodbye to everyone," she tells her little sister. Rachel must be brave, for now she is going to have to look after Esther. When the war is over Rachel wants her parents to be proud of her.

Mr. Pear takes Esther's other hand. "Come on, Maaike," he says. "We're going by car. Look, there it is, in front of the door."

"Oh, boy!" Esther shouts. "We're going in a car!"

The girls give everyone a kiss. Rachel notices that her

mother's hands are ice cold. "Goodbye," Mother whispers to her.

The girls stand in front of the door. Rachel feels the wind on her face. She would like to keep standing there, for she has not felt the outside air in such a long, long time. Rachel finally turns around to wave at the window where those left behind are standing and watching.

"Get in," Mr. Pear calls to them.

❖   *A New Uncle and Aunt*

Yesterday Mr. Pear brought Rachel and Esther to a new household. "Welcome to Venhuizen. I am Aunt Nel and this is Uncle Jaap," the woman of the house had said. "You are our children now."

Nowadays the girls get new aunts and uncles without any more ado than that. It takes a while to get used to saying aunt and uncle instead of Mr. and Mrs.

The children will no longer be sleeping in a hallway as they did at their previous address; here they will be sleeping together in a bed in a real room.

"Do you think that these people are nice?" Esther asks.

"I think so. They were nice yesterday evening, anyway.

The man has an especially nice face," Rachel answers. The girls are relaxing and chatting in bed, now that it is morning. They are not going to get up yet, for the woman said that she would come and call them to come downstairs. In the meantime they are playing all sorts of games.

"I spy something green," says Esther.

"Grass," Rachel replies.

"Silly, there isn't any grass here."

"There is outside."

"Maybe we'll be allowed to go outside here," Esther speculates.

"Yes, maybe."

The girls hear someone walking up the stairs. The woman comes into the bedroom and opens the curtains. "Tomorrow we'll have to open the curtains earlier, for the neighbors have already come to ask if I have guests," she tells them. "Here in the village everyone pays attention to everyone else, and no one must know that you're here."

"Of course not," says Esther.

"When you're ready you may go in the back garden for a little while."

"See?" Esther claps her hands. "Didn't I tell you?"

The man and woman have already had their breakfast, so the girls eat alone.

"I like it here," Esther announces.

"That's fine," says Aunt Nel. "Come on, you may go outside." She opens the door.

Esther remains in the kitchen. "May we really go out?"

"Of course."

"What about the Nazis?"

"There aren't any Nazis here today," Aunt Nel explains, "and if they do come, we'll hide you better."

"Where?"

"I'll tell you about it later."

The girls are standing outside now. They can see the pasture from the garden. Everything is green.

"How beautiful it is," Rachel whispers. "There is the sun and there . . . I see houses way in the distance. May I go inside now?"

"Are you afraid?" asks Aunt Nel.

"Yes, very afraid."

When Uncle Jaap returns from work in the afternoon, Aunt Nel tells him that Rachel and Esther had been in the garden. "Ria was afraid," she says. "The poor child didn't dare remain outside."

"How long has it been since you've been outside?" Uncle Jaap asks Rachel.

"A long, long time, more than a year," she answers.

"I'll bring along a reed mat from work," Uncle Jaap promises. "We'll put it around the garden and then you won't have to be afraid anymore. We have to get some sun on those little white faces of yours."

Rachel looks at Uncle Jaap. "You are a nice man," she says.

❖ *Roundup*

"Do you know what a roundup is?" asks Uncle Jaap when they are at the table eating their lunch.

"Yes," says Esther. "The Nazis come to look for you and when they've found you, you have to go with them and then they beat you up."

"That's almost right, little maid," says Uncle Jaap. "It does mean that they look for people who are in hiding, but it also means that they simply arrest people on the street. 'Halt, come with me, you're arrested,' they say then. If there is a roundup, you must hide behind the cabinet in the parlor. I'll show you what I mean."

Uncle Jaap goes with them to the parlor where they always drink coffee on Sundays. "Here is the cabinet," he says, pointing. "You must hide here and be very quiet. I have to tell you this because it is for your own good."

"For my own good, too?" Esther asks.

Uncle Jaap smiles. "Yes, for your own good, too. Do you know what the Nazis do sometimes? When they suspect that people are in hiding somewhere, they go inside. They turn the whole house upside down, and if they cannot find any people, they sit very quietly in a room for a while. They wait until the people in hiding give themselves away by making noise. Sometimes they shoot through walls and cabinets."

"What scary stories, Uncle Jaap." Rachel shudders.

"They are scary, but unfortunately it is necessary to tell them to you," he explains.

"May we go into the cabinet now?" asks Esther.

"Yes, do that for a little while. Wait, I'll go first." Uncle Jaap taps against a wooden wall that is the back of the cabinet. The wall opens like a door.

"Go ahead," says Uncle Jaap. "When you have crawled behind the wall, set it in place and no one can see that you are sitting back there. That way it will be very safe."

They do what Uncle Jaap has said. First Esther goes into the cabinet, then Rachel. It is very dark. By groping Rachel sets the wall back just as Uncle Jaap explained. "And now sit quietly," she says to Esther.

They do not say anything to each other. They sit and wait.

They hear Aunt Nel washing dishes. They hear Uncle Jaap whistling a song.

After an hour Uncle Jaap calls them. "Come on! Put

the wall aside. You have practiced for fifteen minutes. That is enough now."

"Fifteen minutes!" the girls exclaim when they are standing in the room again. "It was an hour."

"It seems like it. It was just fifteen minutes. You were perfectly quiet, really perfectly quiet."

"I never want to go into that cabinet again," Rachel says.

"I hope that you never have to," Uncle Jaap answers.

Yet they do have to. Uncle Jaap comes home from work all out of breath. "Quick, behind the cabinet. There is a roundup!" he calls.

They rush to the cabinet. They know exactly what they must do. Uncle Jaap takes the rear wall away. "Quick," he whispers. "Remember, don't move and do be quiet. I'll call you when everything is over."

Esther is already behind the cabinet. Now it is Rachel's turn. She crawls inside. Her hands are shaking so much that she almost sets the wood back in the wrong place. She puts it back correctly nevertheless. The girls sit down.

"Ow, you're sitting on me," whispers Esther. "Get off of me."

"Shhh!" Rachel puts her finger to her lips, but she knows that Esther cannot see that in the dark.

Hand in hand they sit very quietly. They hear the sound of an auto outside. Twice they hear an automobile door being closed.

"There they are," whispers Esther. "I have a stomach-ache."

"Quiet!"

The bell rings. Rachel hears Aunt Nel walking to the door and then voices speaking in German.

"No," says Aunt Nel. "I haven't seen them. They must be somewhere else."

"Nazis," cries Esther. "I hear Nazis."

They hear the outside door close.

"They're inside, Rachel. They're inside."

Rachel squeezes Esther's hand. Esther squeezes back.

It is very still in the house. They don't hear anyone. "They're inside," Rachel thinks. "They're going to shoot through the cabinet now." She feels her whole body beginning to shake.

Then . . . a shot.

"No," Rachel cries out. "Don't shoot. Take us. Here we are. In the cabinet."

There is a knock on the wooden wall. "Shhh," calls someone, and then Uncle Jaap's voice: "Hold on a little longer!"

The girls are sitting dead still now. Rachel feels that she has gone to the bathroom in her pants, but she doesn't care. She would like to keep sitting here until the war is over.

There is a knock on the wall again. "You can open the door!" calls Uncle Jaap.

They don't move.

"Come on, it's safe now."

Rachel takes the wood away. The children are so stiff that they can hardly get out of the cabinet. Hand in hand they stand in the parlor.

"Whew," sighs Uncle Jaap, and he wipes his face with a handkerchief. "It almost went wrong. Luckily they didn't come inside."

"I heard shooting," Rachel says. Uncle Jaap does not answer.

"I heard shooting," Esther says, too.

"That's right," says Uncle Jaap. "At Farmer Laan's, two houses from here, there was also a Jewish girl in hiding. They shot her."

Uncle Jaap weeps, and Rachel and Esther weep with him.

❖ *Holy*

Rachel has read many beautiful books about saints while she has been in hiding. She has read about Saint Bernadette, Saint Joan of Arc, and Saint Theresa. Rachel would like to be as holy as the saints, but she is not a Catholic. There probably has never been a Jewish saint.

"I want to become a Catholic," she tells Aunt Nel.

Aunt Nel is very surprised. "Do you mean that?" she asks. "All right, the priest knows you're here. We'll ask him if he can come tonight and talk about it."

"I want to become a Catholic, too," says Esther.

"All right, we'll talk about you, too," Aunt Nel promises.

In the evening the priest is sitting with them in the kitchen. "Ria and Maaike want to become Catholic," Aunt Nel informs him.

"That is a good choice," the priest nods. "I'll go talk to your parents tomorrow. You'll hear from me after I've spoken with them."

The next day they talk about baptism. "Just this once you may come to church with me," Aunt Nel says. "And I'm going to shine your shoes, and you'll wear flowers in your hair."

The girls are very cheerful at the thought of it all. Being in hiding and yet going outside — how can that be?

"When I'm baptized, I'll become holy later on," Rachel says. "Just like Bernadette and Joan of Arc and Theresa."

The priest returns, bringing a sad message with him. "Their parents don't want them to be baptized. 'Later, when they can choose for themselves and if they still want to,' their father said."

Rachel weeps bitterly. There goes the outing to the church. There go the flowers in her hair. And she can't become holy, either.

"I see that you're crying," says the priest. "That's good. You are now martyrs for the faith. Before Saint Bernadette and Saint Joan and Saint Theresa were canonized, they were martyrs; now you are, too. Aunt Nel told me that you pray every day. Keep praying."

"Amen," says Rachel.

"Amen," says Esther.

❖ *Rita*

Rachel dreams about Rita. She sees Rita almost every night. They play together then, they talk, they laugh together.

Rita was her best friend when Rachel was still allowed to be in the same class with non-Jewish children. Rita sat next to her at school until the Nazis put a stop to that.

When Rachel is awake she no longer remembers what Rita looks like exactly, but when she dreams she can even see the birthmark on Rita's cheek. Rachel likes to dream about Rita, but sometimes it makes her very unhappy. She yearns to really see Rita and to touch her.

It is Sunday, and they are all sitting in the parlor. Today is the one day the girls are allowed to look outside. The parlor window sill is full of flower pots; all sorts of plants are arranged neatly in a row — red flowers, purple ones, white ones. Esther and Rachel may kneel in front of the window and peek outside from among the plants. In that way no one can see that they are there.

Rachel and Esther spend the whole week looking forward to Sunday, for that is the only day they can see people up close.

"Look, a child," Esther exclaims. "She's dancing with a piece of rope in her hand."

"That's called jumping rope, Esther. Don't you remember that anymore?"

"No," whispers Esther. It is very strange. When they are looking out from among the flower pots, they always speak in whispers; it makes it seem as if people really can't see them, then.

"In half an hour everyone will be going to church," Aunt Nel tells them. Aunt Nel knows that the girls enjoy watching the people, for there is a lot to see.

The half hour passes quickly. The first churchgoers walk past the window.

"Look, Esther, what a crazy hat that woman has on. It looks like a cake."

Esther laughs.

"Shhh, not so loud, Maaike," warns Uncle Jaap.

Rachel is feeling a bit stiff from all the crouching

down. She stretches her back, taking care not to let her head come up above the window sill. Imagine if someone should see her!

It is very quiet in the street now. Uncle Jaap is sleeping and Aunt Nel has gone into the kitchen to prepare dinner. Soon the girls may peek out the window to see the people coming out of church; after that their Sunday watching is over for another week.

Rachel looks into the empty street. How wonderful it would be to go outside! She hasn't been allowed outside for such a very long time. Would it be unpleasant in the sun?

A girl is walking nearby. She has on a coat that is much too big for her. The girl comes closer.

"Rita!" Rachel calls out. "Rita!"

"Shhh, don't shout so," Esther whispers.

"There's Rita! Rita, I'm here! Come on!" Rachel wants to knock on the window pane, she wants to shout, but she does neither; she lets herself fall at full length on the floor. "Rita!"

Uncle Jaap has awakened. "What's the matter with you?" he asks.

Rachel points to the window. "Rita!" she shouts.

Uncle Jaap runs to the kitchen. "Come quickly, Nel," he calls. "Ria has gone crazy!"

"What's the matter?" Aunt Nel asks as she comes into the parlor.

"There," Rachel sobs. "There is Rita."

"Who is Rita?"

"She's my friend from Rijswijk. I want to play with her."

"Poor thing," says Aunt Nel. "She's sick. Children can go crazy from years of sitting inside. She thinks that she sees a friend from Rijswijk."

"But isn't that true?" asks Uncle Jaap.

"What, have *you* gone crazy, too?" Aunt Nel says to him.

"But it's true," he says. Rachel sees that Uncle Jaap is startled.

"I forgot to tell you," he explains. "Yesterday evening some children arrived here from Rijswijk. There is no more food for them in that part of Holland."

"Rita!" Rachel calls out. "Rita. Here I am!"

❖ Grandpa and Grandma Will Write Tomorrow!

"Just a couple more hours," says Aunt Nel, "and they'll be here."

"How many is a couple of hours?" Esther asks.

"About two, Maaike," Aunt Nel replies.

"That's terrific!" Esther cheers. "In about two hours my father and mother are coming to visit."

The time has finally come when the moon isn't shining. The Hartogs may visit each other only when it is completely dark outside. One month Papa and Mama can come to the De Langes' house, the following month the girls will go visit Papa and Mama.

Aunt Nel has baked cookies for the occasion. She still has a bit of real tea on hand, and she plans to serve it tonight.

"You have to have something special for important company," Uncle Jaap explained. "You have to give important company real tea to drink, not imitation tea. That imitation tea is rubbish."

"Good evening, everyone!" Father and Mother are already standing in the kitchen. No one noticed their coming in.

"Hello, everybody. Hello, children." Mama looks at Rachel and Esther from head to toe. "You've grown again, Ria. How is it possible in one month."

"Won't you call me Rachel, Mama? I don't like the name Ria."

"All right, but softly then: hello, Rachel."

"Hello, Mama."

"Go sit down, people. It's wonderful to have you here," says Uncle Jaap. He pulls two more chairs up to the table. Now there are six people sitting in the warm kitchen.

They drink tea and eat cookies. How cozy it is. If only it could stay like this!

Papa is quieter than usual tonight. Could he be sick?

"Are you sick, Papa?" Rachel inquires.

"Why do you ask?"

"I don't know. Because you're not saying anything."

"No, I'm not sick."

"Ria has knit a pretty blue sweater for herself," Aunt Nel tells them. "Why don't you go upstairs and get it, Ria?"

Rachel stands up and walks toward the corridor. When she has reached the stairs she feels someone pulling on her skirt. She looks behind her. It is her father. "What is it, Papa?"

"Stop," he whispers. "There is something I have to tell you, but remember, Mama mustn't know. I'll tell her after the war."

"What's the matter, Papa?"

"Grandpa and Grandma have been caught, together with Annie and Trijn."

Rachel sits down on the step. "No," she says. "Tell me you're joking. It's not true, is it?"

"It's true."

"They'll never come back. They're already so old." Rachel is weeping.

Father takes out his handkerchief. "Quickly, dry your tears. We have to go back in again. For God's sake, control yourself. Mama mustn't notice anything, and don't tell Esther about it, either. You're big enough to know. Uncle Jaap and Aunt Nel already know about it, but they wanted me to tell you myself."

"Why did I want to go upstairs?"

"You were going to get your sweater."

"Oh, that's right."

"What a clever daughter I have," says Mama when Rachel comes into the kitchen with the sweater. "I never knew that you could knit so beautifully."

"I knit a whole lot," Rachel replies.

They talk about various things. They talk about the war and about the peace that will come one day. They talk about the tea and about the delicious cookies.

"What a good time we're having this evening," Mama remarks. "And I have such a happy feeling. It's been a while since I've had a letter from my parents. I feel that I'll get a letter from them tomorrow, or maybe the day after tomorrow."

"Come, Ruth, we have to go." Father stands up. "Goodbye, Nel, thank you for the cookies and for the real tea. Goodbye, children, see you next month."

❖ *Hello, Esther*

Esther has been very unhappy these days. She wants to go to Papa and Mama. When she lies in bed in the evenings she says the strangest things. "Tonight when you're sleeping, Rachel, I'm going to open the window and slide down the rain pipe. Then I'm going to Papa and Mama. I know where they are. At Aunt Geertje's and Uncle Piet's house."

"Don't you dare! You'll be caught."

"No, I won't. God will protect me. Aunt Nel said so herself."

"Don't you dare!"

What is Rachel to do to get Esther to think of something else? Esther already begins having these strange ideas during the daytime:

"When nobody is looking, I'm going away.

"One day I'm going to disappear."

Aunt Nel comes into the kitchen. "I have to go shopping for a little while. You'll take good care of each other, won't you?"

"No," says Esther.

"Esther, when the war is over we'll go play outside and then we can also go live with our own father and mother again," Rachel says, trying to comfort her.

"When? Next week?"

"No, I don't think so."

"Who are we going to play outside with?"

"With our own friends."

"What are their names?"

"Pietje and Grietje. Jansje and Hansje. Nora and Dora. Now you think of some."

"Tineke and Barend and Poopie and Pissie."

"No," says Rachel patiently, "it has to rhyme."

"Oh, Tineke and Lineke. Joke and Toke. Bessie and Jessie and now I'm going to go to the bathroom."

"All right, go ahead. Will you come back quickly?"

"When I'm finished."

It is taking a long time for Esther to return. Rachel should look to see if her sister is crying. Esther often cries when she is on the toilet; Esther has told her so herself. Rachel walks to the hallway. The bathroom door is open.

Rachel walks in. The bathroom is empty! Esther is gone. Surely she has run to Papa and Mama. It will be Rachel's fault if Esther is caught. She didn't watch her carefully enough. What is she to do, and what will Aunt Nel say?

Rachel sees that another door is open, the door to the street. She will have to go outside and look for Esther. Rachel steps outside. There is Esther, standing very still on the garden path. She is looking up at the sky with one hand over her eyes.

"Come inside, Esther!" Rachel calls to her.

"I'm not going to run away, after all," says Esther. "God can't protect me because He doesn't exist. Otherwise He would have looked at me through a cloud and said, 'Hello, Esther, are you there? How fine to see you outside, too!' "

❖ *Almost Free*

"I think . . . I think . . ." says Uncle Jaap.

"What do you think, Jaap? I'm not in the mood for any riddles," replies Aunt Nel.

"I think that the end of the war is at hand," answers Uncle Jaap. "There's something going on."

Rachel is sitting with a book in her lap, but she isn't reading it. Imagine that Uncle Jaap is right and that it will all be over.

"In six days it will be the tenth of May," Aunt Nel says, with a sigh. "It will then be five years since the Germans invaded our country."

"When it is the tenth of May again we'll have gained the victory. We'll have thrown all the rotten Nazis out by then," Uncle Jaap exclaims.

Rachel has never heard Uncle Jaap talk in such a feisty way before. "Esther," she says cheerfully, "in a little while we'll be able to go outside again."

"Us, outside? But we can't because of the Nazis."

"Uncle Jaap says that the war will be over soon. Didn't you hear that?"

"No, I was reading."

"Oh."

"Ladies, your attention!" Uncle Jaap calls. "I'm going to listen to the radio. Maybe they can tell us more from England."

For as long as Rachel and Esther have been hidden by Aunt Nel and Uncle Jaap, they have been able to listen regularly to the news from England. Up-to-date reports have been broadcast throughout the war in all sorts of languages, including Dutch. "This is Radio Orange, the voice of the fighting Netherlands!" the announcer says at the beginning of each broadcast. The Nazis have forbidden the Dutch to listen to the news from England, therefore Uncle Jaap's radio is well hidden in a cabinet up in the attic.

"Let Uncle Jaap go upstairs by himself tonight," says Aunt Nel. "The three of us will do the dishes. It is already eight-thirty. When Uncle Jaap comes back downstairs we'll be finished."

*   *   *

Aunt Nel washes the dishes. Rachel and Esther dry them. "Well, well, we're almost through, girls. Thank goodness." Aunt Nel empties out the water from the dishpan. "Finished," she says. "Let's wait for Uncle Jaap now."

They do not have to wait long for Uncle Jaap. He comes down the steps making a great deal of racket, and stands in the kitchen with both arms raised up high.

"It's over!" he cries. The Germans have capitulated." He grabs Aunt Nel and lifts her up. "We're free, Nel! We're free! Let's go outside!"

Uncle Jaap opens the front door and shouts, "People, people, come look! Who have Jaap and Nel had in their house for such a long time without your knowing it? We've had Ria and Maaike, two Jewish girls, and we've saved them! We've saved them! Today you can see them outside — Rachel and Esther Hartog, for those are their real names!"

Uncle Jaap stops shouting. He is very still now. He is stooped over and his hands are covering his eyes. What could be the matter with him?

"I'm not going outside," Esther resists. "I don't want to."

"You are free." Uncle Jaap stands upright again.

"Let them alone, Jaap. Perhaps they'll want to go outside tomorrow," says Aunt Nel. "Girls, girls, how happy I am that those rotten Nazis didn't . . ."

"Look, what do we have there? Look outside, children. No, come over here, in front of the window." Rachel and Esther stand at the window of the front room, and what do they see? Papa and Mama are walking outside, right out in the open!

"Papa, Mama!" Rachel rushes outside. Her parents stop short when they see her. They hug each other, they laugh, they cry, they do everything at the same time.

"Where is Esther?"

"Esther didn't want to come outside, Mama. She's afraid."

"Let's go see Esther now," says Father, and he runs toward the house.

"Papa! Mama!" Esther has come outside, after all.

"We're free! Free!" their mother shouts. "We're no longer in hiding."

Together they walk back to the house, where Uncle Jaap and Aunt Nel are sitting at the kitchen table. "Welcome to Free Venhuizen," Uncle Jaap jokes.

"Jaap, Nel, you have saved our children. How can I ever thank you?" Father says.

"Don't thank us," Aunt Nel answers. "If you feel that you have to be thanking someone all the time, you'll never really be free. Come, let's go take an honorary stroll through the village together."

"I'm not going," says Esther. "It's still a little bit light outside."

❖ *Goodbye, Venhuizen*

"I don't want you to go," says Aunt Nel. "We've gone through so much together, and now we have to say good-bye. I wish the car would come and get this over with, already."

The car that is to take the girls back to Rijswijk is an hour late. Saying farewell is becoming even more difficult, now that they must wait so long.

The children said goodbye to Uncle Jaap this morning. They stood and watched him until he disappeared around the corner. It seemed as if he was pedaling faster and faster on his green bicycle. At the corner he looked back one more time, and then he was gone.

Rachel and Esther are now ready to go back to their father and mother, who left three weeks earlier. They do not know which house they are going to. Father and Mother are living in the home of a man whose wife died while they were in hiding. Mama can take care of her own family and the man and his little daughter, too. Mama has written all of this in a letter to them.

"When the car comes I'll help you get in and then I'm going," Aunt Nel says. "I can't stand to see you leave."

"We'll come back soon, Aunt Nel," Rachel promises. "And maybe we won't like it in Rijswijk. Then we'll come back to Venhuizen for good."

"Sweet girl," says Aunt Nel. "Goodness, there's the car."

Rachel is startled. They must say goodbye now. Saying goodbye is surely something that settles in the stomach, for Rachel can feel the unhappiness stabbing her there.

"Goodbye, my little dark-eyed one." Aunt Nel lifts Esther up.

"I'm staying here," cries Esther.

"Go on." Aunt Nel gives Esther a little push.

"Goodbye, Aunt Nel, and many thanks again," Rachel says.

Aunt Nel does not answer; she stands very still on the gravel path, then walks toward the driver of the car. "Sir," she says, "will you drive carefully? We have protected these two little brunettes in order to return them to their parents safe and sound."

The driver looks at Aunt Nel. "Don't you have a handkerchief, ma'am? Here is mine." He puts a red handkerchief in her hand. "Here, keep it. I understand. I hid people, too. We are colleagues, so to speak."

Aunt Nel laughs.

"That's what I like to see," the driver says. "I have to pick up more children who were in hiding and return them, but whether it is to their parents or not . . . I don't know!"

"I'm leaving! Goodbye, girls!" Aunt Nel begins to walk away.

"Goodbye, Aunt Nel," the children shout.

"There she goes," says Esther, "all alone."

"Pray for your aunt," says the driver. "Come on." He starts the engine.

"Goodbye, Venhuizen," the children call out. "Goodbye for now."

❖ *Return*

"Hello, sir, I'm Ria," says Rachel to a man who is standing at the entrance of the house where their father and mother have been living for three weeks now.

"Silly girl, your name isn't Ria anymore," Mama reminds her.

"Oh, that's right. My name is Rachel."

"And I'm Uncle Barend," the man introduces himself. "This is my daughter, Betty. I hope you can get along well together. Luckily your parents and I get along just fine. They have a roof over their heads and I have someone who can take care of Betty and me."

Betty nods.

"Supper!" Mother calls out after the girls have examined the house. "Come to the table, everybody! Rachel, you sit there and Esther, you sit there." Mother points to the other side of the table.

"I want to sit next to Rachel, Mama."

"All right, go ahead."

Rachel and Esther sit next to each other at the table.

"Enjoy your food," Uncle Barend says. "Aren't you going to begin, children?"

"We still have to pray," Esther explains. She crosses herself and folds her hands.

"Pray?" Uncle Barend looks wide-eyed at Esther.

"Yes, pray," Esther answers. "We always prayed when we were living with Uncle Jaap and Aunt Nel. In the name of the Father and the Son and the Holy . . ."

"That's enough, damn it!" Uncle Barend slams his hand against the table. "You are Jewish children. No one in my house is going to pray in a non-Jewish manner. Have you lost your minds? I've forbidden Betty to pray like that, too. Have we come back from hiding to pray as *goyim*?"

Esther is still sitting with her hands folded, but Rachel is so startled by Uncle Barend's anger that she has unfolded hers.

"Enjoy your food," Uncle Barend says again, and he puts a big piece of potato into his mouth.

When their father and mother bring the sisters to bed in the evening, Esther says, "Uncle Barend is a horrible man and I think this house is small and nasty."

"Shhh, don't talk so loud," Mother tells her. "Uncle Barend is pitiful. His wife died while they were in hiding. He doesn't mean any harm. And now let's be happy that we can put you to bed ourselves after so many years. Let's not ruin it by complaining."

"Do you remember how I used to put you to bed?" asks Father.

"I don't think so," Esther answers.

"You both stood up in bed, and then I blew you down."

"Oh yes, that's right. Shall we do it again?" Esther is already standing on the bed.

Father puffs out his cheeks. "One, two, three," the girls count. They feel Father's blowing and then let themselves fall.

"Just like we used to do," Father says. "How is it possible!"

Betty comes in dressed in her nightgown. "I want to sleep with those two girls," she says.

"All right," Father tells her. "Get in this bed. When we want to go to sleep, we'll bring you to your father's room. We'll sleep in here with our children. And now close your eyes. Good night."

"Good night!" the girls call.

"Who would have thought that I would ever again be able to put my own children to bed myself," Rachel hears her mother say.

"Good night!" Father calls out from the hallway.

"How old are you?" Esther asks Betty when Father and Mother have gone downstairs.

"I'm nine years old and I don't have a mother anymore. She died during the war and she's buried in the garden of the house where we were in hiding. It was too dangerous to bring her to the cemetery. When I had just come back to Rijswijk I thought it was terrible that my mother was so alone, lying in that garden. But I don't think it's so bad anymore because before I go to sleep I pray for her. She can hear me from heaven."

"Pray? But your father doesn't let you pray, does he?" Esther asks.

"No, I do it secretly."

"How do you pray? Jewish or Catholic or Protestant?" Rachel inquires.

"Catholic, I think, just as you did when we were going to eat."

"Then we'll pray for your mother with you," Rachel decides. "In the name of the Father and the Son and the Holy Ghost . . ."

"Pray quietly," Betty whispers. "When we pray Jewish we'll do it out loud."

"Hail Mary . . ."

"Shhh!"

❖ Hollands Spoor Station

"I know it for sure," says Mother. "They're coming today. I feel it, Rachel."

Rachel does not believe it. It has already happened three times that they went to the train station in vain to pick up Mama's parents. Grandpa and Grandma must come from the concentration camp Theresienstadt to The Hague by way of Eindhoven. A letter from the Red Cross read something like this:

"You should report to the back of the Hollands Spoor Station."

Now that Rachel has been there three times, she understands why the people from the camps are not permitted to arrive at the front of the train station. Ordinary people would be shocked. She has seen them — thin people, gray people, sick people, and even little people who are the same age as she is herself.

Rachel will go with her parents one more time — then never again. She wants so much to be there when Grandpa and Grandma arrive. She wants to participate in their homecoming.

"Come, we'll go to the train station again," says Father with a sigh.

Rachel walks between Father and Mother. It is wonderful that she can even go outside. Now it's hard for her to imagine that such a short time ago it was forbidden.

The tram brings the Hartogs from Rijswijk to The Hague. They stop close to the station. They walk to the back of the building, and Rachel sees what she has already seen three times now.

A man is sitting at a small table with a big sheet of paper in front of him. He has a gold fountain pen in his hand. Presently he will cross out the names of the people who have arrived.

The Hartogs wait silently. They hear the sound of a train in the distance. "There they come," says Mother softly.

Rachel looks at her mother. She knows how it feels when after a long time you will see your parents again, even though returning from a camp is very different from returning from hiding.

The noise of the train becomes louder. Now not only can they hear the train, but they can see it as well. It stops with a sort of loud sigh.

The doors open. There they are again. People in strange clothes that are too large or too small for them.

"There!" Rachel shouts. "Grandma!"

"Where?"

"There, Papa. That woman with the white kerchief 'round her head."

Papa watches unhappily. "That isn't Grandma. Grandma is much bigger."

The little woman calls out something, but they cannot understand very well what she is saying, and to whom.

"I believe that she's calling me," says Mother. "Yes, she is. Listen!"

"Ruth, David, Rachel!" they hear.

"It *is* Grandma. It is my mother!" Mama is dancing on the middle of the platform. She wants to run to her parents, but she is held back by a policeman.

"You'll have to stop, ma'am. First the people must be registered there at that little table." He points to the man with the gold fountain pen.

It is almost Grandpa's and Grandma's turn. They can understand each other well now, even though they have to shout loudly.

"How are you doing?"

"Fine."

"Where is Esther?"

"At home."

"Really? She wasn't caught, was she?"

"No, thank goodness."

They keep shouting to each other. They cannot wait.

Grandma comes to them with wide-open arms. "Thank God, here we are again," she sobs.

Grandpa walks behind Grandma. "*Hinennie,*" he says solemnly, and Rachel remembers that it's what he used to say. It is a Hebrew word and it means: "Here I am."

They talk, they laugh, they cry. Rachel tastes salt on her lips. Salt from tears. She doesn't know whose tears they are.

"Come," says Father. "Let's go to Esther. We live together at Barend's house. You can live there, too."

"Welcome," calls Uncle Barend when they are standing by him in the hallway. "Go inside. Esther is coming. She is away for a little while."

"Go sit down. I'm going to spoil you, dear parents of mine." Mama looks very happily from Grandma to Grandpa. She can't stop looking at them.

Rachel looks at Grandma, too. Shouldn't Grandma want to take that white kerchief off her head? She knows that Grandma has very pretty hair. She remembers how pretty Grandma's hair looked when she had braided it. She did that only at night when she went to bed. During the day Grandma wore her hair in a knot somewhere on her head.

Rachel goes to sit in Grandma's lap. She strokes Grandma's cheek. "Come here with your ear, Grandma. I want to say something in your ear."

Grandma bows her head toward the girl. "Don't you want to take off your kerchief?" Rachel asks. "When it's on it's just as if you'll be leaving right away again."

"I do want to take it off," says Grandma. "But you mustn't be frightened."

Grandma loosens the kerchief. Very carefully she lets it slip onto her shoulders. Then Grandma looks directly at Rachel. "I was terribly sick and I had lice. They shaved my head. That's why I'm so bald."

Rachel strokes the stubble on Grandma's head. "It doesn't matter, Grandma," she says. "When you've been bald, your hair will be much prettier when it grows back."

"Is that really true?" asks Grandma.

"I know it for sure," Rachel replies.

❖ *Toys*

The Hartogs have been living with Uncle Barend and Betty for three weeks. The house is small, and it is crowded now that Grandpa and Grandma are living there, too.

"Today I'll go to the mayor to try to get a house for ourselves," Papa says.

"And what about us?" asks Grandma.

Rachel sees that Grandma is a bit uneasy because she doesn't know where she and Grandpa are to go.

"You'll live with us. I'll never abandon my parents," says Mama. "Now that we have found each other after so much misery, we'll stay together. We'll ask the mayor for a big house."

Papa has gone to ask for the big house.

"I hope that he gets one," Uncle Barend complains. "It's too crowded here with all these people. I feel like I'm in hiding again. When we were in hiding we didn't have enough room, either."

"It's going to be all right," Father reports when he has returned from his visit to the mayor. "We're going to get a splendid house. During the war an N.S.B.-er lived in it. The N.S.B.-er is now in prison and when he gets out he'll have to look for another house. They won't throw us out, in any case. The mayor has promised us that. And I have a surprise for you, children. You won't believe your ears."

"Oh, tell us, Papa," Rachel begs.

"There are a whole lot of toys in the house, and you may have them because your own toys were stolen by the Nazis."

"Hooray! We're going to have toys again!" Esther claps her hands.

"Dolls, very pretty ones, and teddy bears and a doll-house. I've never seen such a beautiful dollhouse. It must have ten rooms in it," Papa exclaims.

"Go get it now," Grandpa urges. "I don't want to meddle in your affairs, but . . ."

"Pa, I'm not a Nazi." Father is becoming a bit angry.

"I'm not going to take anything out of a house that doesn't belong to me yet. If I did that, I'd be just as bad as the Nazis. We can trust each other again, Pa. We are no longer in a concentration camp."

"Fine, fine," Grandpa mutters. "And yet I think . . ."

"Let David alone, Pa," Mama says to Grandpa. "I haven't interfered, either. He'll take care of everything."

"Here is our new home," Father announces the next morning when they are standing before a large house. "Go inside Pa, Ma, Ruth, children."

They enter a long hallway. "What magnificent marble," Mama whispers. "We've become distinguished people, all of a sudden."

"And now to the toys. Come with me," says Father while he walks up the stairs.

When they reach the top he opens a door with a big sweep of his hand. Esther is the first to go in. Father and Mother follow her. Rachel is still in the hallway when she hears her father talking very loudly:

"That can't be! Everything is gone, the dollhouse, the dolls, the bears, everything!"

Rachel enters the room along with Grandpa and Grandma. Papa is standing there while Mother and Esther are sitting on a bed.

"Damn it, they won't even let my children have toys," Papa fumes.

Rachel feels sorry for Papa. "It doesn't matter," she comforts him, and she strokes his hand. "I still have a book. You know, the book I always had with me when I was in hiding."

"I have a picture book, too," Esther adds.

"You are both so sweet," says Father.

"Didn't I tell you?" Grandpa exclaims. "No one is to be trusted. Not even in Holland." Grandpa walks out of the room. "I'll wait downstairs," he says.

❖   *Grandpa Takes a Walk*

Grandpa has not been able to sleep late since his return from the concentration camp. It used to be very different; whenever Rachel slept at her grandparents' house, Grandma had her get Grandpa out of bed. When the child called, "Get up, Grandpa!" he would pull the covers over himself, grunt a bit, and sleep some more until Grandma came and called out, "Get up, you lazybones!" Only then would Grandpa get out of bed.

Now he gets up at five o'clock every day. He takes a walk then, every single morning. Rachel has asked him if she might go with him, but it seems that Grandpa is alarmed by her question. "No," he says. "Don't come. It's not good for little girls."

Rachel can't understand why he says that. She had to stay inside for such a long time when she was in hiding. *That* was bad. Fresh air is very good for young girls, isn't it?

"You mustn't ask Grandpa anymore about going with him," Grandma said to her. "Grandpa doesn't like it."

"Why not, Grandma? What is Grandpa doing then?" Rachel asked.

Grandma didn't answer. Rachel will never ask again. Her grandparents are acting so strangely. It must have something to do with the camp.

Grandpa left early again this morning. The family usually waits until he is back before they eat breakfast, but he is taking a very long time today.

"Go on and eat. Don't wait for Grandpa," Mother says. "Otherwise you'll be late for school."

Rachel helps herself to a slice of bread and takes a big bite of it. How good bread tastes when it is spread with butter and syrup.

"There he is!" Grandma calls.

Grandpa is in a hurry. He rings the doorbell about ten times. During the entire time he has been living with the Hartogs he has never behaved this way.

Grandpa is standing inside now. He is soaking wet. Water is dripping from his hat onto his shoulders, yet he is smiling.

"Take your coat off, Pa, you're getting everything wet." Mother helps Grandpa with his coat. "How did this happen? It's not raining. What have you done?" Mother asks.

Grandpa does not answer. "Come," he whispers to Rachel, "come, Granddaughter, Grandpa has something delicious for you. Go to the table and don't look until I've counted to three."

Rachel does what Grandpa asked. She puts her hands over her eyes. She hears the rustling of paper and feels Grandpa approaching her to put something on her plate.

"One, two, three!" he calls out.

Rachel looks. Next to her own slice of bread is something that resembles bread, but it makes her feel sick to her stomach. She runs to the bathroom and vomits into the toilet.

From outside the room Rachel hears Grandma speaking very loudly: "Damn it, you've got to stop! You're no longer in a camp. We're back in Holland. You don't have to eat any moldy bread here."

When Rachel dares to go back into the room she hears Grandma telling Mother, "In Theresienstadt he spent fourteen days in a prison cell because he stole bread, and he still can't keep from stealing it here. What are we going to do with him?"

"This afternoon I'll take him past all the bakers of the village," Mother promises. "Then he can see with his own eyes that there is bread for sale again."

When Rachel is on her way to school, Lia comes and walks next to her. Rachel does not really feel like talking. She is preoccupied with thoughts of her grandfather, but she doesn't dare to tell Lia that she would rather walk to school alone.

"I laughed myself silly," Lia begins. "Every morning a dirty little old man comes into our back garden. He opens our garbage cans and takes things out. Then he claps the lids back on again. Today my father threw a bucket of water on him, and when the man comes back tomorrow, I'll be allowed to do it."

Rachel turns to Lia with two fists raised. "You let him alone! Let him alone! Do you hear me?"

Lia looks at Rachel in surprise, then begins to laugh. "Since when do you feel sorry for little old men?" she asks.

"Since . . . since . . . this morning," Rachel answers, and then runs away.

"She's out of her mind," Lia says out loud, and points to her forehead.

❖ A 78366

The house is becoming more and more full. A week ago Miep came to live with the Hartogs. Miep has returned from Auschwitz. "So, here I am. You don't have a representative from Auschwitz yet, do you?" she joked, and then she came inside. "I'm back. We'll talk only about pleasant things," she said to everyone, and they all agreed to abide by her wishes.

Miep sits next to Rachel at the table. She always puts her arm next to Rachel's plate. Rachel keeps looking at the arm because there is a big blue number painted on it: A 78366.

"It's not painted," Miep explained to Rachel when she asked about it. "The Nazis pricked my arm with a hollow needle which had a sort of ink in it. When they needed you, they called out your number. We no longer had names. And now let's talk about pleasant things."

"Yes, Miep," Rachel answered, although by then she was feeling sick from talking about Auschwitz.

Tomorrow she and Miep will be going to Scheveningen. Rachel is looking forward to the trip, but what will it be like to sit in the tram together? Is everybody going to be looking at the number? What will people think? Miep will be the only one with a number on her arm.

An idea comes to Rachel when she is lying in bed that evening. Tomorrow she is going to have a number on her arm, too. Tomorrow morning after she has washed she will take her pen and prick numbers on her arm. Rachel sets the pen and ink pot right by her bed.

The next morning Rachel comes out of the bathroom early. She sits on her bed, takes the lid off the ink pot, and dips the pen into the blue ink. She then begins to prick the A on her arm. Now and then she shuts her eyes because it hurts, but she doesn't mind the pain; the Nazis hurt Miep much more than that in Auschwitz.

The A is finished. Now come the numbers 7, 8, 3, 6. Rachel makes the last number a 4; it doesn't have to be exactly the same as Miep's number. After the ink has dried, Rachel puts a sweater on. No one may see what she has done, except for Miep, of course. Later, when they are sitting together in the tram, she will take off her sweater and say, "Look, Miep, I have a number, too. You're not alone anymore."

At breakfast Rachel sees that Miep has a sweater on, too. She has to laugh a little about that. "Let's eat quickly, Miep. Then we can leave right away."

"Enjoy yourselves," Mother tells them. "You can finally do that again."

When they are sitting in the tram, Miep takes her sweater off. Rachel's eyes focus immediately on Miep's arm. The number . . . where is it?

Rachel looks at the other arm. Perhaps it is there; perhaps she has not looked hard enough.

There is no number on the other arm, either.

Miep points to a bandage. "I've covered up my number," she says. "Not everyone has to know that I was in Auschwitz."

❖ *Mrs. Van Dalen, Remember?*

One day Aunt Jetje, who also lives with the Hartogs now, comes home very forlorn. "It happened again," she says. "I've had enough of it."

"Don't let it bother you. People in Holland don't know any better," Grandma says, trying to comfort her. "You're not accustomed to being questioned, but that's because you've just come back from the United States. We're already a bit used to it."

"Must I keep telling people that Annie and Bram and little Ineke were killed?"

"Yes, there's nothing else you can do."

Rachel has been sitting and listening very quietly to the conversation. She feels tears coming to her eyes, but she is able to hold them back. Rachel knew Annie and

Bram, who were Aunt Jetje's daughter and son-in-law. Ineke was Aunt Jetje's granddaughter.

Rachel will try to cheer up Aunt Jetje, if she can. She has promised Mother to do the shopping. Perhaps Aunt Jetje would like to go with her.

Aunt Jetje would like very much to accompany Rachel. They walk arm in arm along the Haagweg. "Just as I used to walk with Annie," Aunt Jetje remarks. "That was pleasant, too."

Rachel chatters without stopping. She must do her best not to talk about the time she spent in hiding. Aunt Jetje must be comforted, but Aunt Jetje asks so many questions.

"How did you feel the first time you had to go out on the street with the star on your breast?"

Rachel doesn't answer.

"Child, what did you do all those years when you couldn't go outside?"

Rachel doesn't answer. How can she explain her feelings to someone who was in the United States during the entire war?

"Hello, Mrs. Nieweg!" A woman is standing in front of Aunt Jetje. "Don't you know me anymore? I'm Mrs. Van Dalen, remember? I used to wait on you in the store."

"Oh, yes," says Aunt Jetje; but Rachel sees on her aunt's face that she doesn't know who the woman is.

"How are your — "

"Fine, fine. Annie and Bram and little Ineke are fine. They are living in a splendid house in Florida. They even have a swimming pool. Goodbye, Mrs. Van Dalen. Come, Rachel, let's keep going."

Aunt Jetje pulls her along, but Rachel can nevertheless hear Mrs. Van Dalen say, "There goes another Jew who should have been gassed. Horrible show-off. She won't talk to a shop assistant anymore."

❖   *Uncle Jacob*

Rachel loves Uncle Jacob very, very much. She hasn't seen him in three years. One morning he was taken from his home by the Nazis. Her cousin, who was twelve years old at the time, opened the door, and when they shouted out to the boy, "Where is your father!" he answered, "He's here in the house." They went upstairs and took Uncle Jacob with them, one Monday in May.

Now that the war is over, Rachel waits for Uncle Jacob every day. Mama's parents have returned, Aunt Liny and Uncle Jo have returned, Miep has returned, and now it is time for Uncle Jacob to return.

Grandpa and Grandma, Father's parents, will not be returning. Mother told her so, and Rachel has gradually come to realize it herself. Each evening she hears Papa crying about his parents. She hears him when she is lying in bed, and deep down under the covers Rachel weeps, too. She pities her father and her murdered grandparents.

"It will happen tomorrow. He'll come tomorrow," Rachel thinks every day, and therefore every day she wants to wear her prettiest clothes.

When he does come, he will call to her just as he used to do: "Hello, my little dark-haired girl, come to your uncle." He will lift her up and hold her very high above his head and she will scream, just as she used to do, "Put me down! Stop! Stop!"

Uncle Jacob will be coming today. Rachel wants to put on her white blouse. "Mama, where is my white blouse?" she calls downstairs.

"On the big bed. I still have to iron it."

"Don't bother, Mama, I'll do it myself." Rachel takes out the ironing board. In the linen closet is the flannel sheet that must be put over the board. She opens the linen closet door; the sheet isn't there. Is it on a higher shelf, perhaps?

Rachel takes a stool and stands on it. She can look very high in the closet now. She sees a blue-flowered tablecloth that she can still remember from the time before they went into hiding. That cloth was always laid on their table when someone in the family had a birthday. The last time it was used was when Esther turned eight years old.

Rachel puts her hand on the tablecloth. There is a crackling noise, the sound of paper rustling. She lifts up the cloth. A stack of envelopes is lying among the blue flowers. Where has she seen these before? She knows; on the doormat. Those envelopes with a red cross on them have been put through their mailbox almost every day this week. Has Mother hidden them in the linen closet? Why?

Rachel takes an envelope and carefully pulls a letter out. There is much to read on the paper. Her eyes skim over the lines. Mother must not know that she is doing this. She will have to read quickly. At the bottom of the letter are the names of Papa's parents and then:

> PRESUMED DEAD IN SOBIBOR
> ON 10 APRIL 1943

Rachel is startled. Even though she knew about the deaths of her grandparents, this information from the Red Cross makes it seem so very certain now.

Rachel puts the letter back into the tablecloth and takes another envelope. She opens it and reads:

> JACOB ROZEBOOM
> PRESUMED DEAD IN MAUTHAUSEN
> ON 30 NOVEMBER 1942

Rachel begins to laugh. The Red Cross is crazy. Her Uncle Jacob dead? Of course he isn't; he'll be coming back today or perhaps next month. He is somewhere in Russia and he has lost his memory. Next month he will know who he is. He will come in and call out to her: "Hello, my little dark-haired girl, come to your uncle."

Rachel irons her white blouse on just the wood of the ironing board. She puts it on and stands in front of the mirror.

"How pretty he'll think I am, and how grown up I've become," she says to her reflection.

❖ *Is Old Jopie Still Around?*

These days Rachel no longer knows whether a person is alive or dead.

Each time that people who have been in hiding or in a camp get together, she hears: "Is he still around? Is she still around?"

All too often the answer is "no." That is the reason Rachel never dares to ask about anyone. Sooner or later she learns about the person in question, anyway.

Today is Friday. On Friday the Hartogs always have lots of visitors. They celebrate the beginning of the Sabbath together with many people, just as they used to do before the war. It is almost as cozy as it used to be, yet it is very different; there is no longer so much laughter.

"That old Jopie was a funny man," Grandpa says in the evening. "Given the chance he would always be teasing someone."

"Is he still around?"

"No."

"Aunt Mietje could sing beautifully. She was in a choir."

"Is she still around?"

"No."

Mother shows her guests a photograph. "This photo was also in hiding," she jokes.

"Oh," says Papa, "look, Uncle Louis and Aunt Eva. And there, by my finger, are Leo and Leny. They're all dead." The photograph is put back in the drawer, and they continue to converse and to tell jokes.

"If they just wouldn't start talking about people again," Rachel thinks, "then maybe they would keep telling jokes the whole evening."

"Say, have you heard anything from Professor Van Dam?" inquires Grandma between jokes. "He was with us at Westerbork."

"Is he still around . . .?"

"I'm going to bed," says Rachel.

"Already?" asks Mother.

"Yes, I'm tired." In bed Rachel can think about whatever she wants and does not have to keep hearing that one question: "Is he still around?"

In the street the next day Rachel meets the nursery school teacher. Years ago she thought that Mrs. Van Arum was very nice. When Rachel stayed in Rijswijk with her aunt and uncle, she was often allowed to go to nursery school along with her little cousin. She would then be placed in Mrs. Van Arum's class. Rachel remembers that she found the school in Rijswijk much more pleasant than the school in Rotterdam.

"You've gotten so big," exclaims Mrs. Van Arum.

"Yes," says Rachel.

"You haven't had an easy time, have you, Rachel?"

"No, ma'am."

"Do you remember Tineke and Michel?"

"Yes ma'am, Tineke had long braids."

"You have a good memory," the woman remarks.

"Is she still around?" Rachel inquires.

Mrs. Van Arum looks at Rachel. "Now why would you ask me that?" she says.

❖ Green Beans

Grandma and Grandpa have brought everyone a gift from the concentration camp. There is a nail scissors for Father, a ring for Esther, a bracelet for Rachel, and a silver pan for Mother.

"I found these items among the things that people left behind when they had to go to another camp," Grandma tells them.

"Are those people dead, Grandma?" Rachel would like to ask, but she doesn't dare. She thinks it is horrible to have to wear something that belongs to a dead person. That is why she has never worn the little bracelet made of blue beads.

"Aren't you going to wear that pretty bracelet?" Grandma asked her.

"I'm afraid it will break, Grandma," Rachel answered. She can't say to Grandma that she doesn't want to wear that nasty bracelet, can she?

Father uses his nail scissors and Esther wears her ring. Grandma thinks that is quite nice. "All that misery, yet I brought gifts back with me," she says, and then she looks very happy.

So far, Mama has not set the pan on the table. Thank goodness! Whenever Rachel sees it in the kitchen cupboard, she cannot help thinking about the people who had it on their table long ago. In what country might that have been?

They are sitting at the table. Grandma comes in with a platter full of potatoes. Mother carries a small platter of meat.

"Wait, I'll get the green beans," Grandma says. "Stay in your seat." Grandma is already on her way to the kitchen.

"Mmm! Green beans," Esther calls.

Now comes the moment that Rachel has been dreading. Grandma comes in with the pan. "Here are the green beans," she says cheerfully. "I've scrubbed the pan inside and out. Isn't it lovely?" She places the gleaming pan in the middle of the table.

"Rachel, go on, eat," Papa urges. Rachel takes a piece of meat and some potatoes.

"You must take some green beans. There are a lot of vitamins in them. They're good for you," says Mother, and she comes toward Rachel with the pan. "Come on, Rachel, you have to take some green beans."

"No."

"No? You've always liked green beans."

"Not anymore."

After dinner Rachel and Esther wash the dishes. They do this each evening. The girls sing while they work and have a lot of fun together.

Rachel has no desire to sing tonight. "Go bring the cups that have been dried back to the parlor," she says to Esther.

The washing up is almost finished. Only the pan is left. Rachel dips it into the soap suds. "Miserable pan," she whispers. "I'll fix you." She opens the kitchen door, takes the pan, and with a giant heave she throws it over the wooden fence that surrounds the garden. "So, that was that. No one ever comes back here in the pasture. We'll never see that pan again."

"Children, thanks for doing the dishes," says Mother when she comes into the kitchen. "Look, look, you're almost finished putting everything away. That's fine."

The following evening at the dinner table Grandma says, "I've looked high and low for that pan I brought for you from Theresienstadt, and I can't find it anywhere. Does anyone know where it is?"

"I don't," says Mother.

"I don't," says Esther.

"I don't, either," says Rachel.

❖ Almost Free

Rachel had such high hopes of going back to school. It has been three weeks now since she stepped once again into the building from which the Nazis had expelled her.

She is no longer able to learn. Geography is not going well, and arithmetic is not going well, either.

Fractions? Never heard of them.

Multiplication, division? Never heard of them.

"If you can't learn, you'll have to go to the school for housekeeping when you're out of grade school," Mother often says.

But what is Rachel to do at the school for housekeeping? She is not handy at all. She doesn't use a vacuum cleaner properly or wash dishes well, either.

Writing essays is wonderful. During the time she was in hiding Rachel invented many stories. They are inside her head, and all she has to do is to write them down.

If only Rachel's arithmetic were a little better. Mr. Stigter is a very nice teacher. He helps her with her sums even after school, but he can't do much about the fact that she doesn't understand anything, and that she has become so stupid.

* * *

"Children," says Mr. Stigter when they have hung their school bags on their chairs. "Children, get ready to write. We're going to write an essay."

"Thank goodness, no arithmetic," Rachel says to Lineke, who sits next to her.

"We're going to write an essay about a very fine subject," Mr. Stigter continues. "We're going to write about the liberation that we went through such a short time ago. I'll give you forty-five minutes. Get to work!"

Rachel bends over her writing. So, the title of the essay is already there: "Almost Free."

She will begin with the evening before the liberation, and gradually tell some more about the fifth of May, Liberation Day. Rachel writes the first line under the title:

" 'I think . . . I think,' says Uncle Jaap . . ."

Uncle Jaap, Aunt Nel, how are they doing? Aunt Nel was terribly sad when they left Venhuizen. Has she gotten over that sadness by now?

Rachel bites down on her pen holder. Splinters of wood come on her tongue. She spits them out.

"Can't you do it?" Mr. Stigter puts his arm around her. Rachel feels his head close to hers.

"No, sir, I can't write anything more."

"Why is that?"

"I don't know."

"Are you crying?"

"No."

"Come with me. We'll go to the teachers' room together." Mr. Stigter turns to the class. "Children, I must leave with Rachel for a while. Keep working. You still have half an hour."

Together, Mr. Stigter and Rachel walk through the long corridor. Their footsteps sound loud against the stone floor.

"Go in." Mr. Stigter holds the door open for her.

"Now I'm not good at language anymore, either," Rachel says, sighing.

"Of course you're good at language," Mr. Stigter replies. "We know that, don't we, but do you know what I think? Perhaps it is still too soon for you to be able to write about the liberation. You still have so much to digest. I hope that I may help you with that."

"Yesterday evening it came to one hundred five!"

"One hundred five?"

"Yes, each evening my father and mother count how many family members are gone."

"Killed?"

"Yes. Seventy-three from Mama's side, and tonight it's Papa's turn to count again."

"Here," says Mr. Stigter. "Here is my bread ration I have brought to eat during our break. Go outside and give it to the ducks. Go count how many ducks are swimming

in the water. Thirteen-year-old children should be count-
ing ducks, not dead people."

"May I go outside, just like that? My essay isn't finished."

"Go on, go on. I don't care. You may give them all my
bread. Feeding ducks during school time and feeling the
sun on your face. That is freedom, too. And that essay
. . . Perhaps you can write it some day when you have
been in middle school for a long time, or in high school,
or even later. I won't be your teacher then, but may I read
it, anyway?"

"Of course," Rachel answers.

"Promise?"

"Promise."

"Do I have your word for it?"

"You have my word for it."

❖ "Gone"

One hundred thousand Dutch Jews were killed in German concentration camps. Among them were the following people mentioned in this book:

Uncle Jacob   *in Mauthausen*
Herman   *in Auschwitz*
Aunt Esther   *in Treblinka*
Uncle Max   *in Treblinka*
Mirjam   *in Sobibor*
Sally   *in Sobibor*
Grandpa and Grandma Hartog   *in Sobibor*
Max   *unknown*
Lex   *unknown*
Riwkah   *in Auschwitz*
Benny   *in Theresienstadt*
Marga   *in Bergen-Belsen*
Mientje   *in Bergen-Belsen*
Johnny   *in Auschwitz*
Aunt Malli   *in Auschwitz*
Uncle Maurits   *in Auschwitz*
Bram   *in Sobibor*
Annie   *in Sobibor*
Ineke   *in Sobibor*
Old Jopie   *in Treblinka*

Aunt Mietje   *unknown*
Uncle Louis   *in Auschwitz*
Aunt Eva   *in Auschwitz*
Leo and Leny   *in Auschwitz*
Professor Van Dam   *unknown*

Father Thijssen was imprisoned in Scheveningen. He was released five months later, on Hitler's birthday.

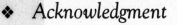

❖ Acknowledgment

I have tried to record our experiences as accurately as possible. However, in the course of this book I have named only four hiding places.

Many other people sheltered us for one or more days and nights, but it would have been unsuitable for the story to mention all the people and all the hiding places.

My decision to omit names for literary purposes does not change the fact that these people helped to save our lives.

Ida Vos